CO-AUTHOR

CO-AUTHOR

A PARANORMAL THRILLER

ARTHUR MILLS

Branching Plot Books

2015

5900 Balcones Dr, Ste 5650, Austin, TX 78731
www.branchingplotbooks.com

Library of Congress Cataloging-in-Publication Data
Mills, Arthur.
Co-Author A Paranormal Thriller / by Arthur Mills.
2015902969

ISBN: Paperback   978-0-9891840-8-3
ASIN: eBook for Kindle   B00WTGYZWC

BOOKS BY ARTHUR MILLS

The Empty Lot Next Door
The Crawl Space
Friend or Foe
Co-Author

CHAPTER 1

"Chelsie, where are you?" she heard Brian ask excitedly.

"I'm in the living room," she responded nonchalantly.

"Look what just arrived in the mail. It's your latest romance novel!" Brian rushed into the living room, nearly tripping over the rug.

Brian handed the book over to Chelsie with shaky hands. Without looking at the cover, she placed the book on the coffee table and returned to looking out the window.

"Honey, it's your new book. Aren't you a bit excited?"

"Why should I be? I already know what it looks like."

"This is your ninth romance novel. Like all the others, this one will be a big hit."

"You remember what Kimberly Chase wrote in her book review, 'Chelsie Crammer is just another regional author,'" Chelsie said while still looking outside.

Brian sat down next to her. "Just another regional author? That's crazy! You're the number one best-selling romance writer in the Pacific Northwest. That's not small potatoes. You've influenced the romance fiction market in our area like no other author. All that in just seven years! Besides, America is a huge country, honey. Even Robert Frost and Harper Lee were often identified as regional writers. I think you're in elite company."

"But the Northwest can't be the definition of my readership. I want more, my readers want more," Chelsie responded.

Of course, her image contributed to her success as much as her talent – she was well aware of it.

Chelsie was beautiful, very beautiful. She had the height, the proportions, and the looks to be a successful model – and the narcissistic attitude to carry that image with impudence. On the insistence of a friend, she did a few modeling assignments while at college. But they never really interested her. The dreamy final images that ultimately emerge from a photo shoot never reveal the mundane business of the actual shoot. Chelsie enjoyed flaunting her beauty in real life – but a photo session wasn't the right place for her. Holding a pose stiff and upright for ten minutes while numerous adjustments were made to her arms, hair, shoulders, breasts, and hips turned her off. Of course, she understood modifications were necessary, but they killed her spontaneity. And since childhood, Chelsie had been nothing if not spontaneous.

Feeling a little better, Chelsie finally looked at Brian, "But I haven't written a real masterpiece yet. I want to be the next best thing."

Picking up the book, Brian said, "What are you talking about, Sweet Surrender will be your masterpiece." Chelsie's good feelings dissipated, and she looked away again.

Losing the struggle to cheer up his wife, Brian leaped from the couch and grabbed her laptop. "See, look here. Look at this review from The Seattle Times. They say Sweet Surrender is the best Chelsie Crammer Romance novel to date. It says here, it's a standard masterpiece."

"If it's standard, how can it be a masterpiece?" she asked.

"Well, different people set different standards. To your regular readers, this book will deliver everything they expect from you. They'll spread the word, insist their friends read it, and be proud to get their copy of the latest Chelsie Crammer romance signed. Weren't these exactly what Steinbeck and Faulkner also expected from their readers?" Brain said in a careful voice.

Chelsie didn't respond as she watched the late winter afternoon dissolve away.

In a last-ditch effort to help his wife feel better, he set the laptop down and picked up her new novel. "Your fans will love the cover. Your protagonist is muscular and handsome."

Chelsie turned from the winter wonderland outside and looked at the handsome man on her cover. A smile finally materialized on her face.

The guy took her in. He was a strong man, not meaningless bulk of muscle but real strength — a broad frame, sculpted chest, and powerful shoulders. Not like Brian at all! Sure, she and Brian were extremely emotionally and physically compatible. Yet he was never the man Chelsie's fantasies were made of. Fantasies were an integral part of her existence and a major inspiration for her novels. Chelsie was naturally gifted with writing, but she'd never explored much beyond her imagination for subjects to write on. It was her strength and her limitation as well. Her rich and vivid imagination, a keen understanding of the psychology of love, and vivid descriptions of love scenes had endeared her to thousands of readers. She'd never tried to break this comfortable mold. Why should she? Her first nine books sold well, she had loyal followers, and her publisher regularly pressed her for new manuscripts. Life was good at thirty-two, and she was thankful for it.

Holding her ninth book, Chelsie considered the reviews published in local newspapers and journals. They were mostly positive, as expected, and she knew this title would sell equally well. Most of her author friends had already read it and praised it. Brian, her most dependable critic, had also vetted it.

Becoming a writer hadn't been her goal, but she did love literature. At one point, she had thought of becoming a university teacher – teaching English literature seemed an excellent way to stay connected with creative people. But majoring in English literature had robbed her of the charm. This was the problem with her. She would set high ideals and standards, but once she got to know something inside out, she'd find shortcomings she was unwilling to live with. She taught Creative Writing for a couple of years at Evergreen State College in Olympia, Washington, while drafting her first novel – The Rose. Surprisingly, she hadn't faced rejections and stonewalls. The first publisher suggested several changes to her manuscript, which she found most logical, and resubmitted the draft after making the alterations. Soon after, her book was published. It took just three months to reach the top of the charts. She had engaged an agent since, and publishers were now only too eager to publish a Chelsie Crammer Romance.

She left the teaching job after her second novel was well-accepted. That was the year she married Brian, a local newspaper correspondent. They had known each other since college. He was a great person to be with. Most importantly, he understood Chelsie. She had never felt more comfortable with another person. He was warm and wise, while she was emotional, whimsical, impulsive, and even narcissistic. It was difficult for Chelsie to believe someone could relate to her fantasies and even encourage her to fantasize actively. Brian proved to be a perfect partner – emotionally and physically.

Chelsie widened her smile as she looked at Brian. Brian, feeling victorious, grinned.

Chelsie loved his grin. It was warm and open and transformed his appearance. Because going by accepted standards, Brian's physical appearance left a lot to be desired. He neither had a muscular physique nor was his face attractive. His hair was usually unkempt, and he wore thick glasses that made his eyes look nerdy. Many of her friends thought them to be an impossible couple. There was a time when they used to wonder openly how Chelsie – with her much-desirable body and a greater-than-average sex drive – could remain satisfied in this relationship. But Brian's attitude towards life made him an excellent companion. Not only was he witty, well-read, and insightful, but he also made up for his lack of a chiseled body with his eagerness to play with her in bed. Chelsie considered herself lucky to have a husband who could ably support her in intellectual and erotic pursuits. Brian understood Chelsie's physicality, and erotic fantasies channeled themselves through her writing.

"Forget what Kimberly Chase wrote in her review. Maybe she's threatened by your success. So don't worry about it. You're *my* favorite romance author. How about a little sweet surrender right now?" Brian stared at Chelsie's perfect body frame.

"No sweet surrender until tonight!" she shot back with a laugh.

CHAPTER 2

Rrring. Chelsie rushed to answer the phone.

"Hey, you rock! Sweet Surrender is great." Amy said unceremoniously. "I think it's your best work yet."

"I agree," said Linda on the three-way line.

Amy and Linda were Chelsie's best friends. They had been together from school – sharing influences, ideas, good times and bad. She could confide in them without the anticipation of any biased judgment. To them, she wasn't a bestselling author; she was a friend whose well-being – not image – was their primary concern.

Chelsie couldn't join in their enthusiasm with equal vigor.

"That's not what I think," she said.

"Why? We liked it so much," Linda said.

"Don't you think it's exactly like all my other books?" asked Chelsie.

"Of course it is. It has everything in it that you always write about." Amy tried to sound reassuring.

"That's exactly the problem," Chelsie replied.

"Why don't you like it?" asked Linda.

"It's not specifically about the new book. I'm unhappy with all my nine books."

Linda whistled in surprise.

"Chelsie, you're crazy. You're so talented," Amy chimed in.

"I'm troubled," Chelsie continued after a long pause, "not because my books aren't being appreciated, but because they're being appreciated by the same set of people – or so it seems. Look, America is a large country. I want to reach out to more people… to other parts of the country… to be regarded as a real author. Not just a regional one."

"So, write a book everyone will read," Amy said casually.

"Do you mean everyone doesn't read Chelsie Crammer's Romances?" Linda confronted Amy.

"Depends on how you define 'everyone,'" Amy tried to reason.

"I need to get more attention from areas outside the Northwest. I need to write a juicier novel… much more romantic than anything I have written. Something people will sit up and notice and something to make me an American author."

****

The thought egged her day and night, so she discussed it with her agent, Kevin Firth.

Kevin was quick to realize her agony.

"You're ready for a bigger playing field," he said. "Now you need to gather all your skills and work towards a plan. You need to get out of your shell and put more into your work."

"More of what?" she asked.

"Of everything, I suppose." Kevin smiled. "Expansion is the key. To broaden your reader base, include new settings, places, people, and…" Kevin paused.

"And?"

"… and new romance!"

"What do you mean by new romance? I do that in every book I write," Chelsie said defensively.

"No. You write about the same romance under different names. Be it The Rose, the Queen of Hearts, The Moonlight Sonata, or Sweet Surrender, you're simply repeating a winning formula. Your dedicated readers love it, and you'll always have your own market; that much is assured. But if you're genuinely concerned, you must get some fresh air in your writing. That would blow away labels."

His words seemed logical, yet Chelsie was doubtful.

"How fresh can romance get?" she asked. "It has remained the same since a hundred ships set sail for Troy!"

"True," Kevin agreed. "But you might bring in different things."

"Introduce different erotic games? There is a limit to the human anatomy, Kevin. I mean, how innovative can you get without bordering on the bizarre or the grotesque? I write romance novels, not porn! Besides, the generally accepted normal descriptions are basically repetitive."

"Not when you do it in different settings," said Kevin.

Chelsie waited for him to elaborate.

"Do you get my point? You need to engage new readers who can relate to the settings of your novels. For that, you need to write about different settings. Get out of your 'urban girl meets rich-but-young brat and reforms him through true love' mode, and you'll draw new readers. To attract Pan-American attention, you must get more of America in your writing."

"Do you mean literally? Explore new places and surroundings, or just new styles of writing?" Chelsie was curious now.

"Perhaps both. A change of place is always a good idea. It stirs your brain up. Regarding style, I leave that to you. But, of course, you can always spice things up a little more. Even a 'Bad Sex Award' sells, you know?" Kevin winked.

****

That evening, Chelsie told Brian everything Kevin had said.

Brian nodded. "Sounds sensible. Nine novels on similar themes should be enough for a writer to think about a change of scenario. Try something different for your tenth, honey! Let's rent a country cottage amidst nature."

"You really think so?"

"Of course! I was thinking about a career change myself. This job as the local correspondent is getting stale. I want to do something more meaningful. It would be great to change my surroundings."

"Hope you're not thinking of a changed marital status?" Chelsie giggled as Brian lunged at her playfully.

She eased herself into his tight embrace. The thought of a fresh start seemed appealing. Her worries were beginning to melt away. Of course, she can do it. She will bounce back with a grand tenth novel, and the critics will be compelled to sit up and take note.

"Why don't you start writing books, too?" she murmured as Brian fumbled with her top.

Co-Author

"Too much competition at home!"

CHAPTER 3

They spent almost the entire spring searching for a suitable country cottage – like two birds building a nest – and summer was knocking at the door when they decided on their perfect abode.

First, they decided on the kind of place they wanted to live in. Both agreed there should be a lake and a forest in the vicinity. Next, Brian began researching cottages of the sort that were available. He had very particular specifications in mind regarding aesthetics and functionality. He wanted a large front porch overlooking a garden or a landscaped courtyard. He said this would link the outdoors with the home's interior and aid Chelsie's imagination while writing. He also wanted details like gabled roofs, dormers, windows with small panes, fireplaces, wooden floors, and an all-brick facade. Finally, Chelsie had to put a leash on Brian's enthusiasm.

"This way, we'll never get our country cottage. Settle for something livable and affordable – that's all."

"Well, I would have settled for a log cabin," he said apologetically, "but I want a comfortable setup for you."

Kevin had helped her secure a handsome advance for the tenth Chelsie Crammer Romance. He was pleasantly surprised that Chelsie and her husband quickly accepted his advice for a setting change. Kevin had been Chelsie's agent since her second book, and they shared an excellent professional relationship. He was on the other side of fifty and harbored somewhat fatherly affections for the talented and cheerful young couple. Kevin was now family.

"This would be easy to sell," he had said to her, laughing. "Publishers should queue up to sign on a Chelsie Crammer novel that will exude the raw vitality of rural romance."

"Don't expect Lady Chatterley's Lover!" Chelsie had warned.

"And why not? This could be the book to catapult you to nationwide recognition."

Her publisher, Will Black, was hopeful about the forthcoming title but curious about their move to the country. He was doubtful whether the urban spirit Chelsie embodied and was so well-accepted among young adults wouldn't be dampened because of this shift. Nevertheless, Mr. Black agreed with Kevin, who emphasized Chelsie's need to break the mold. Rural romance may be a more lucrative business proposition since urban romances were currently a dime a dozen. Experimental work by an influential writer always had a chance of winning some high-brow award and helping his publishing house project a distinguished profile.

"You need the right place to create the right ambiance," Mr. Black said. "But that will depend on your luck. Unless you go and settle in a place, you never know what it will be like."

"It's not really about my liking the place," Chelsie had replied. "All I hope is that the place is capable enough of stimulating new ideas. It's all Kevin's brainchild, you see. And Brian thinks it's worth a try."

"Anyway, I have nothing to lose," Mr. Black announced. "Either devise a Chelsie Crammer Romance that breaks new ground or turn in a modern-day Walden. Both could create ripples if positioned with tact in the market."

"Exactly!" Kevin was overjoyed that Mr. Black had so succulently summarized his point. "Her tenth must be memorable."

****

Brian's persistence paid off, and they finally settled on a cottage. Although the porch and the courtyard weren't as large as he wanted, the cottage exuded a kind of cozy elegance neither of them could ignore. Brian resigned from his job at the newspaper to arrange for the move. His editor was initially incredulous.

"What do you plan to do in the country?" he asked Brian.

"Just roam around, I guess." Brian winked.

"It's not even a place I'd ask you to send in news reports from. Why don't you go to a new city instead? Then I could plant you there as my local correspondent."

"Don't want to file any more reports for a while."

"So what exactly will you do while Chelsie writes?" The editor was getting worked up. Brian was a handy employee who never had many demands. He would have liked to retain him at any cost, but he knew that – although easygoing – Brian could be adamant once his mind was made up.

"Read, perhaps," Brian replied. "Or I'll roam around a lot. It's been a long time since I lived amidst nature. My grandfather had a farm I used to visit during vacations, and I have fond memories of it."

Chelsie didn't have many arrangements to make. She was connected to her social circle through the internet, which meant she carried her world around on her laptop wherever she went.

They moved to their new home one bright summer afternoon.

It was in the country in the true sense of the term. Brian had selected a cottage near the nearest town, virtually at the forest's edge. Beyond it laid the sprawling woods. It was a dream come true for Brian. He enthusiastically identified each species: Pine, spruce, larch, fir, juniper, poplar, willow, walnut, birch, chestnut, oak, elm, ash, maple, and cedar. Chelsie was amazed to find an amateur botanist at home. Brian always surprised her with new talents —this was yet another example!

The lake was a short walk from their back door. Its water was still and dark and situated in an area where the forest was sparse. There was even a clearing around it.

"You need to stay for at least a year in a new place to appreciate it," said Brian one morning, a week after they had moved in.

"Sounds like a new theory. Why exactly a year?" enquired a curious Chelsie.

"Then you get to see all the seasons there. I mean, a place being a geographic location, you get its complete look and feel only after you have observed it in all possible natural settings — be it spring, summer, autumn, or winter."

"Not a bad idea. But how long do we intend to stay here?" she asked.

"That depends on you," he replied. You might want to return after gathering enough material. Or you may like to complete your book here. Or… you may want to stay here forever…"

"Forever! Here? Why would I want to do that?" Chelsie exclaimed.

"Why not? Don't you like the place?"

"I do, but I had never considered settling in the country."

Brian was silent. A goldfinch trilled ceaselessly. It was the only noise they heard. Then he spoke.

"I like the silence… and the lake," he said. "It's almost a place where one could stay until the end of time."

"You're too easily impressed!" Chelsie laughed.

The place was okay to her. As picturesque as she had seen in countless movies, nothing could sweep her off her feet. She loved the cottage, however. Brian had an eye for those things. A white picket fence bordering colorful blooms and plants surrounded the one-story, three-room cottage. There was a manicured front yard and an inviting covered porch. The foyer led to a spacious living room with a fireplace. The ceiling had rafters, and the dining area boasted beautiful hardwood floors. The split bedroom plan positioned two bedrooms on opposite sides of the home. Chelsie had converted one of them into a writing studio. The attic, crowning the house, lent a vintage feel.

Despite all her enthusiasm, she was a little depressed. She usually had a jovial personality that received sustenance from urban living. City lights cheered her up more than fireflies did. All her writing described the nuances of city life – people with purpose, urban traffic, plush hotel rooms, contemporary offices, state-of-the-art gadgets, and girls and boys who had been born and bred amidst civilization. Nature was undoubtedly enjoyable in small doses, but Chelsie had never felt the urge to embrace it as a way of living. Of course, as a teenager, she used to get turned on thinking of nature camps – another name for nudist colonies. Her young and responsive body would tremble at the thought of walking around a settlement with all her assets up for scrutiny. This fantasy was valuable enough to melt in a series of explosions under imploring fingers. She had moved on to other fantasies since, and flowers tastefully arranged in vases were more to her liking than flowers in the uncertain wild.

Why had she decided to move to the country then? She was a bit unsure on that one. She wanted to write a great book to shake up her readers. But she was not as convinced as Kevin that such a drastic change was necessary or possible. Nevertheless, it was great to be with Brian out in the wild. That was the only encouraging aspect.

That afternoon, they went for a walk in the woods. As they reached a clearing towards the east of the lake, Brian stopped and pointed at the crimson glow of the westbound sun shimmering on the water. The clearing was a little undulating, covered with soft grass. They stood for a while before squatting on the grass. A strong breeze blew across the lake. The crimson from the sky ricocheted off the lake to paint their faces red. There they sat, man and wife of six years, like a prehistoric couple, by the shores of some pre-Cambrian lake. The sun continued its oblique course, and the breeze grew cooler. Overhead, birds returned to their nests after a hard day's work. They flapped, chirped above the snuggling couple, and descended on trees in the forest behind them. As Chelsie huddled closer, Brian put an arm around her.

"Are you cold?" he asked.

"I rarely am!" she winked. "But it will be dark soon."

Chelsie was feeling good. She had stopped fantasizing since they moved in here. It was perhaps because she couldn't relax in her new settings and constantly felt an inner tension. But today, she felt calmer, and her body seemed to respond to mental cues. She grabbed Brian tighter.

He smiled. "What else do you expect to happen after the sun goes down? Scared of the dark, are you?" he queried playfully.

"Hope we'll be able to find our way back," she murmured.

"There's always an afterglow. Besides, the lake is a good landmark. You can never lose your way here; it's a short walk to our cottage."

Chelsie was neither fearful nor anxious about losing her way with Brian around. Yet she wanted to make him think she was feeling insecure; she was helpless and exposed to the elements and anything that might happen to her in this desolate landscape. The thought set off tingles in her belly, and her body twitched uncontrollably.

She stiffened her muscles and whispered, "Is the place safe?"

"Haven't heard of much wildlife around here," Brian replied.

"People might be more dangerous."

"You're paranoid!" he laughed. "There's no one around."

"Town isn't very far. There might be outlaws who hang around here in the wild."

"Even if there were, what would they possibly do?"

"What not? I'm beautiful and sexy, and you're not carrying a weapon," she purred.

Her tone gave it all away. Brian realized she was in one of her reveries that had made her priceless to him and would soon require culmination in a frenzied play of love.

"Tell me more," he said.

"They could do anything. They might tie you to a tree and force you to witness my humiliation. They could secure me by my arms and legs… yes, arms over my head and legs spread very wide…!" As she spoke, her bosom heaved, and her breathing turned shallow.

"And then?"

"Then the one standing behind me would grab my tits … ooh!" Chelsie squeaked as Brian firmly gripped her bosom from behind. As eager hands roved over her perfect orbs, she panted. "Ooh… Please leave me alone! Nooo… the other one is forcing his hands between my thighs…"

Brian freed one of his hands to reach below. Filling several roles during moments of passion was difficult, but he was no stranger to the game. As he deftly roved over her submissive body, dusk descended on the dreamy landscape.

CHAPTER 4

Brian went around the place regularly; it was his daily ritual. Every morning after breakfast, they'd lounge in the garden for about an hour, and Chelsie would do some stretching and freehand exercises while Brian listened to music on his iPod or just loafed around with a book in hand and chatted. He knew she wouldn't speak while exercising, so it wasn't a conversation, but both enjoyed mornings. They wouldn't have dreamed of such luxury back in the city, where Brian had already rushed to work when Chelsie woke after writing until very late the night before. Here, the mornings seemed to come early, and surprisingly, both had been getting up without any deliberate attempt to alter their lifestyle.

Exercise over, Chelsie would sit at the desk with her laptop, and it would be barely 8:00 a.m. She'd check her inbox, surf, breeze through her social networking commitments, and begin planning her tenth novel. Meanwhile, Brian would set out on his regular expeditions. He varied his route daily to explore different areas in the vicinity, and some days, he would walk in the woods. On others, he would take the bike and pedal aimlessly – randomly visiting the local church, the marketplace, the town nearby, and so on. He took the car only when they needed groceries from town. Some mornings, Brian would walk over to the lake and sit by its side – staring at the dark waters until the sun was above the tallest trees and its rays beat vertically.

After lunch, Chelsie would work until around four in the afternoon and then go for a stroll or sit in the garden until dark. The evenings were mainly reserved for reading and TV. Brian was in the habit of reading until late into the night. He had retained that habit; strangely enough, Chelsie gradually metamorphosed into a morning person. She found it more productive to write during the day. Unlike in the city, evenings she turned into nights early in the country. She discovered the previously unknown pleasure of tucking herself into bed by nine after a good day's work.

About a month into their country exile, Brian returned from his morning expedition early with a sheepish grin writ large over his face.

"I got a job!" he announced.

"As a woodcutter?" Chelsie didn't say jokingly.

"That would be a great idea. Nonetheless, this one is less arduous. I'll be teaching English at the local school. One of the teachers is starting maternity leave and needs a replacement."

Chelsie asked incredulously, "What local school?"

"There's one next to the post office – just behind the square. You haven't been around town much…"

"Not apart from the small department stores."

"Yeah… the principal is nice; I met him at the church a few days ago. What do you think?"

"Well, okay, I was a teacher, and I know you can be great if you set your mind to it. But do you intend to set your mind to it?"

"Umm… I think I'm going to enjoy this. My only concern is that you might feel lonely. School's over by two every afternoon, though!"

"Not an issue. I work later than that. It's you who needs to find something engaging."

"And the money won't hurt either!" Brian winked. "By the way, the principal hasn't ever read a Chelsie Crammer Romance."

"Big deal! How old is he?"

"Nearing his sixties, I guess."

"Doesn't matter," shrugged Chelsie. "I'm sure he'll definitely be interested in them once he meets me."

****

It was the first major change since moving to the country. Although she remained busy writing through the day, she missed having Brian around. She was getting used to their new life – a ceaseless vacation. She was thankful her successes as a popular regional author allowed them the sabbatical.

However, she wasn't very comfortable with the place yet. It was undoubtedly not oppressive; no, she was taken in by its natural beauty. But she felt the place lacked life. Life, to her, was motion, conversation, going places, meeting people, lights and sounds, and the anticipation of something new. Everything in the city was so uncertain; everything here was so sure. And then you had yourself to spend time with – she found out that was not easy. She had glorified action in her books– romantic, sexual, financial, or professional. Her characters excelled in acting out the deepest of their desires. It felt strange to lead a life devoid of anything hasty. It was vegetative, slow, and certain. She knew not how this place could inspire her school of writing. Perhaps she needed to change her schooling altogether – in the way she looked at things and in the way she wrote.

She asked Brian.

"But of course," he said. "You're looking for change – be it your plot, setting, or, if needed, your writing style. You aim to write something more readers can connect to and will contain more of America in it. Since you have decided to go for something new and your publisher is ready to take the risk, you should try something you've never done before."

"It's not that I don't like the place, but I can't find any inspiration in it." She admitted.

"Honey, it's like a relationship. You can go about it in two ways. Either you rush to a hasty one-night stand and then analyze how satisfying the romp was and whether it's worth continuing, or you can take your own sweet time to explore each other – getting to know the person better and deciding whether it would be worthwhile to go to bed at all. A place can influence you only as much you allow it to."

"What does that mean?"

"You haven't gone around the place, have you?" Brian smiled. "Not apart from the walks we've taken together, right?"

"Umm…no, I haven't."

"You need to explore… get to know the place, honey! Start from your immediate surroundings: first the house and vicinity, then the neighbors and, of course, the forest and the lake."

Chelsie was silent. Brian was always so sensible! Although she was more successful, he was her source of sustenance.

"You know what," Brian continued, "there's another small town a few miles away. Let's go for a joyride and check it out. Maybe if you get to know the local life, your creative mind will chance upon things to inspire you."

Brian's enthusiasm was infectious. Chelsie could very well think of a new beginning. After all, one rarely gets the opportunity to begin things afresh. And here was her chance.

She began looking around the cottage with greater objectivity. The place was undoubtedly beautiful. The air was not the same as what she used to breathe back in the city. Not only did it smell different, but it also felt different, too. And then there were the sounds of nature –unlike the urban soundscape. Here, even silence had its own character – distinct and sonorous. Of course, there were chirping birds, the whisper of the breeze, and the murmur of leaves. And on still nights, lying in their bedroom, she heard lake water lapping at the shores in the forest behind their cottage. She needed to get familiar with the locals. The soul of her novels was the people in it. Her critics had always been unanimous in praising how she evoked life's warmth. Chelsie definitely wanted her new book to capture the essence of her surroundings. She decided to go about the place as methodically as Brian had suggested – starting with the house and gradually spreading outwards until she was in sync with the ambiance.

****

It was a Wednesday, and Brian was away at school. Chelsie left her writing desk around ten in the morning. The plot wasn't shaping in a way she liked. Despite all her efforts, she was troubled that her thoughts sought refuge in the old formula that bore the hallmark of a Chelsie Crammer Romance. She needed a break.

So she got up and strolled up and down the hall for a few minutes. It was a glorious summer day, bright and dazzling. The sun warmed the garden all around their cottage. Through the window, Chelsie could see the crest of the tall poplars in the woods beyond. A warm summer breeze swirled around, drawing dried leaves and dust in small eddies and playfully scattering them after a while.

"I'll explore the house!" she thought. It was always interesting to ransack an attic, and she decided it would be the best place to start. She wanted to do this while Brian was away because, in some inexplicable way, she'd have been embarrassed if he were there.

Much to her disappointment, the attic was nearly empty. The previous owners seemed to have cleaned meticulously before they left. But it wasn't bare; a wooden trunk lay under the rafters in the eastern corner. Chelsie pushed it cautiously with her right foot. The trunk seemed full – but not very heavy. No lock was fastened to the latch. Curious, she opened the lid with some apprehension. Men's clothing was inside. Not many, but they were of all varieties: shirts, trousers, jeans, vests, boxer shorts, and briefs. Chelsie gingerly lifted one of the briefs with a finger. Its owner seemed endowed with a physique that had filled the item well. She let it drop inside the trunk with a smirk. She continued to explore the other things. Finally, she took a couple of checkered shirts, one white T-shirt, and a pair of blue jeans and went down with them.

She stood before the full-length mirror in the bedroom and tried on the clothes one after another. She wasn't sure why. Part of her was amazed she was doing it, yet she couldn't resist. She looked in the mirror curiously. The clothes were clean, relatively unused, and well-fitting. They didn't look too bad either. Wearing them, Chelsie felt strangely liberated. She was tall and sturdily built, so she could never wear Brian's clothes. He was a slighter build. But these clothes were perfect for her, as if tailor-made to her dimensions.

She especially liked the green and blue checkered shirt. It accentuated her lovely bosom. Perhaps leaving the top two buttons open had achieved a sensuous effect because desire surged within her. She kept looking in the mirror. Only when the doorbell rang did she realize it was late afternoon. She responded, unmindful of her experimental dressing.

Brian stood at the door. "I forgot my key."

Chelsie giggled like a schoolgirl. As he entered, Brian couldn't help but wonder how much more attractive his beautiful wife looked in men's clothing.

"What are these?" he asked.

"I found clothes in a trunk in the attic," she replied.

"The attic?"

"Yeah."

"Why are you wearing them?" Brian sounded alarmed.

"Just for fun, dear," she assured him as if pacifying a child.

"You might catch a dust allergy." Brian continued.

"From now on, I'm going to dust around and explore the house," said Chelsie with a twinkle in her eyes. "That would clear up a lot of clutter – both outside and inside my mind. Know what, darling? I'm getting the hang of this place at last. Perhaps now I can start working on a fresh plot!"

CHAPTER 5

Exploring the neighborhood was next on their to-do list. But before they could begin, an elderly gentleman visited them with a basketful of local fruits one Sunday morning.

"Hi, I'm William Furlow, but you can call me Bill!" The visitor bowed as Brian opened the door.

"Welcome!" Brian stepped aside. "I'm Brian Crammer. Have I seen you somewhere?"

"Yes, we've met in town, although we didn't have a conversation. I have considered visiting you since I learned you moved in. Just waiting for my garden fruits to attain the right color," The man laughed an open and good-natured laugh.

"Have a seat," Brian said as he pointed to the couch.

They sat on opposite sides and started chatting. "I'm your closest neighbor."

"And that would be…"

"I'm the cottage to the west, just beyond the willows. My compound is large, with a lot of open space, so you would overlook the house from this end. I love gardening, you see. I grow all sorts of fruits and vegetables."

"Yes, I've seen your garden but overlooked the cottage. I thought no one lived within a mile." Brian smiled. He liked the elderly gentleman. The mop of gray hair over the balding head, the eyes glowing with empathy, the white and bushy mustache, and his carefree laughter made him endearing.

"Not within a mile, no! That would be just you guys and me." Bill grunted. "We had the Jones at the cottage to your north. But they moved to Florida some years back…"

As Chelsie walked in, Bill's words trailed off.

"Bill, meet my wife, Chelsie," Brian introduced her.

Bill stared at her for a few moments.

"Hi!" Chelsie smiled as she offered her hand.

Bill seemed to regain consciousness and rose slowly to accept the proffered hand.

They sat down and chatted. Bill was a good speaker, and soon, they talked about Chelsie's profession, Brian's school, the local church, the marketplace, the town, and Bill's late wife.

"The country life is the place to be if you want restful living," Bill declared proudly.

"Country livin' isn't for all," said Brian with a twinkle in his eyes. "Chelsie is a thoroughbred city girl."

"Doesn't matter," said Bill. "I'm sure it will grow on her.

Chelsie smiled. "How long have you been here?" she asked.

"Twenty-two years, to be exact!" Bill replied.

"That's a long time!" Chelsie exclaimed. "You must know the area pretty well?"

"Oh, yes. I've seen people come and go. They often say the country is no longer what it used to be; it has some truth. You know... the sprawl will kill it. The disorganized way the neighborhoods are spreading, without a care for nature or the countryside's rural feel – this reckless development is a shame! And with the burgeoning population, cities, and suburbs will continue to expand in the coming years."

"That kind of growth won't disappoint Chelsie." Brian winked.

Bill turned to face Chelsie. He stared deep into her eyes for a moment before speaking again. "She must be sensitive enough to feel the vibes – or else she wouldn't have been an author. I have a feeling she's going to like this place."

Chelsie smiled yet fidgeted in discomfort. The stare was too incisive. She tried to steer the conversation elsewhere.

"You seem to be quite knowledgeable about the country and not only about this area," she remarked.

"Well, I was a draftsman myself," Bill smiled, "and was quite drawn to the works of Andrew Jackson Downing in the early days of my career. Not sure whether you've heard of him."

Chelsie hadn't, but Brian nodded. "The landscape designer who revived the Gothic style in America."

Bill's face beamed with a grin of amazement coupled with appreciation. "You're well-informed. Downing was a great man... designer, horticulturalist, and writer – who had revolutionized the country living in America. He believed 'every American deserved a good home,' ... that's what he used to say. And when he published his book Cottage Residences – he proved that good living was synonymous with living with nature. His designs blended cottages with their surrounding landscape and natural habitat. That book changed how I perceived good living as an ambitious young professional. I realized how nature can affect your home and health."

Both Chelsie and Brian were engrossed. It was evident that Bill was an expert in his profession. His words were inspirational, and Chelsie genuinely wanted to learn more.

Bill suggested they visit the upcoming county fair in town. He also knew the forest well and the types of trees and birds that could be found there. And then Chelsie asked about the lake.

"Brian is drawn to it, you know. He likes to sit and stare at the water," Chelsie said as she rolled her eyes.

Bill fell silent abruptly and again gave that long, cold stare. Chelsie couldn't help wondering how the man switched between two modes – cheerful, chatty, distant, and troubled. Yet she coaxed him about the lake.

"It's deep!" Bill uttered after some time. It was evident he didn't want to continue on the subject.

They could no longer revive the conversation. While leaving, Bill asked them to visit his place. He glared at Chelsie and walked out of the picket gate.

After he left, Brian kept joking about Bill staring at her.

"He's eager for a Chelsie Crammer Romance – and I don't mean a book!" he guffawed.

She responded with an absent-minded smile. Brian continued to crack lewd jokes throughout the rest of the day.

That evening, as they explored each other like eager teenagers, Chelsie stopped mid-action with a naughty smile.

"You know what?" she said. "That man has charged me up!"

"Who?" Brian asked.

"Mr. Furlow. I mean, Bill. He has stimulated me indeed."

"So your next fantasy will be about elderly gentlemen?"

"You have such a dirty mind!" Chelsie playfully slapped his awaiting organ. "The way Bill described the area has me thinking. I should use all his anecdotes and rearrange my new plot around local life."

CHAPTER 6

David would be the perfect name for the protagonist of her novel. The timeless marble wonder chiseled by Michelangelo epitomizes ultimate male perfection. Chelsie was determined to shape him up with the best of her craft – and words were all she had to create her world of fiction. Michelangelo had a chisel and hammer, yet he hadn't endowed his famous David with as much attribute of maleness as she would have wanted. She'd read somewhere that although Renaissance art paid extreme care to depict the male genitals in all its titillating detail, size was one thing they weren't concerned with. Most male organs in Renaissance sculptures depicted a boring, average-sized, balanced, and well-proportioned member.

This wasn't going to be the case with her David. She would sculpt a real hero with her words – muscular, adorable, and well-endowed. Chelsie remembered the briefs stuffed inside the trunk in the attic and couldn't help but smile. The wearer had stretched the garment to its limits. Chelsie didn't regularly encounter this –

although she had never felt her husband inadequate. Yet size had its attraction and did have a place in her colorful fantasies.

This time, it would occupy its place of pride in the tenth Chelsie Crammer Romance. Until now, although her fantasies had fuelled the plots for her previous novels, she had never really let loose and laid bare her actual fantasies. She portrayed them as inspiration through her rich, multilayered language. It was enough to turn on her young readership. They'd always wanted more, and she had retained the veil of anticipation, but it would be different this time. This would be a much, much steamier novel. She'd use real fantasies – stuff that had stimulated her without fail. Never before had she given them to her readers; Brian was the only one who knew. She was thrilled as she imagined exposing her deepest secrets to the drooling mass. Deep inside, it seemed to satiate some perverse dream and tugged at her creativity both at emotional and physical levels.

She'd had enough of mush and tears for teenagers. Now, she wanted mature men and women to lust after her book. In a way, they would then lust after Chelsie Crammer, the novelist. She would document her inner self, but only she would know the truth. While critics would analyze the turn in her creative persona and readers would repeatedly flip to the back cover and steal a glance at the author's photo – only she would know it was her being felt over and over by the public.

Would Brian know? Nothing was kept secret in their relationship. She was confident enough that Brian would flash his trademark grin and make some witty comment. But, surprisingly, she wasn't entirely comfortable with the thought.

One thing was for sure: this wouldn't be a chicken-hearted urban story. It would be wild and reckless, a rural saga reflecting the grandeur and vastness of the rugged countryside. It must capture human passion like none of her previous novels ever had.

She called her agent that afternoon.

"Hey Kevin, you'll be glad to know that the tenth Chelsie Crammer Romance will fulfill your expectations," she said. "It's going to be wild!"

"Great! So we can expect the next 'Bad Sex Award'?" Kevin said.

"Pity they don't give out a 'Good Sex Award' because it will be good this time."

"You mean 'better'! You were always good at depicting acts of passion."

Chelsie laughed heartily. She was feeling confident and carefree all of a sudden. She knew David wouldn't let her down.

****

Whenever she began a new novel, Chelsie prepared copious notes where she elaborated on the primary characters. She listed personality traits, likes, dislikes, quirks, and tendencies – everything down to the minutest detail. In short, she created a human on paper. Later, when the plot had crystallized, and the turn of events charted out, she put the characters in the envisaged situation and decided upon the most natural response expected from a particular individual faced with the situation. This made writing easy because the narrative took its own course, and, in a way, the novel wrote itself. It was the secret of her warm language and realistic characterization.

As she crafted David, Chelsie found a caring and sensitive man, yet wanted to have rough sex. Despite a very rigid and conservative upbringing, he was wild in the truest sense of the term. He was eternally searching for a partner who would be a gentle and "normal" woman – sharing and caring for her dreams and desires – yet wanted to stretch the limits regarding sex. It was a tall order, as David found out through several encounters. Most girls were indifferent to kinky sex or shocked at the idea. The few women who enjoyed experimental sex were not his type.

With his oversized libido and pristine mind, David was looking for a girl who would match him in the realms of fantasy and the demands of a real, caring relationship. Chelsie thought of several encounters she could script depicting David in his quest. The novel would be steamy indeed, unlike anything she had attempted. The challenge would be to keep things juicy enough without getting raunchy. Chelsie wouldn't want to disappoint her staple readership, who appreciated the right amount of warmth in her novels. Yet she tried to break free of the mold at least for once. Clichéd as it sounded, she wanted to evoke the "fires of passion."

The next day, Linda called.

"How's our country bird doing?"

"Chirping most happily!" Chelsie gushed.

"You sound happy!" Linda was a little surprised. She and Amy had received calls and Facebook posts from Chelsie, and she hadn't sounded overjoyed with her self-imposed rural exile. It was more of a business tour for her, undertaken purely for professional benefits and not passion.

"Yes, I'm happy. I found a great man."

"Wow! Some rustic stable hand, is he?" Linda quipped. "Jokes apart, how's your novel coming along?"

"It's going to be a great book, with lots of sex," Chelsie said.

"That pretty much summarizes all your books – doesn't it?" Linda asked.

"This is different. This will have real sex with a real man."

"Oh, this is the man you've been talking about?"

"Are you disappointed? David is how a man should be." Chelsie announced.

"Tell me more," pleaded Linda.

Linda and Amy had always been the first to hear her plots; in a way, they were her guinea pigs. Chelsie would note how they reacted to each turn and twist and modify accordingly. While Amy was an impressionable reader who got carried away, Linda was more cautious and critical. Both types of feedback had a use, and Chelsie liked sharing the plot with them at an embryonic stage – something most published authors strongly despised. For the ultimate academic criticism, she trusted Brian. Then, it was over to her agent, Kevin.

She told Linda all about David and shared a brief plot overview. Linda was excited, very unlike her.

"This is going to be one bomb of a novel," she said. "A romance that hits hard, and I'm sure more people will sit up and take notice. Now, tell me how the heroine is going to be."

"I have two options there. She could either be a person who fits the bill exactly for David, or she could be totally different and gradually gets around to his way of thinking. I would prefer the first, however. But I might eventually make her a mix of both to build tension and keep the narrative alive."

"Oh, oh! The good girl who gradually sheds her inhibitions?"

"Maybe. There is also a third possibility. She could be the exact type David is on the lookout for: a guy who is decent and responsible, yet wild. And then they meet."

"Fantastic! I think that's how it should go. What's her name?"

"My heroine? I haven't decided yet. I'd been thinking mostly about David…"

"You seem obsessed with him!"

"Oh yes, I am," Chelsie said, pleasure oozing in her voice.

"Why don't you name your heroine Chelsie?" Linda suggested.

Chelsie was silent. It hadn't struck her before, but it seemed a great idea now that Linda had mentioned it. However, she didn't admit it straightaway.

"Oh, come on!" she said coyly.

"Why not?" Linda queried. "I think it's a good idea. Your readers will love it."

Why not, indeed? After they hung up, Chelsie had more or less decided her heroine would be a character who could match David stroke-by-stroke in passion! And wasn't Chelsie that kind of a person? Didn't she harbor secret desires all her life, knowing full well that reality demanded a more balanced approach? Now that she had a chance, why shouldn't she play out her fantasies to the fullest on the pages of her novel – with a companion as able as David?

She was going to be Chelsie.

****

In the evening, she bounced the idea off Brian.

"I'm going to call my new heroine Chelsie," she announced.

Brian was much amused.

"Do you mean Chelsie will be your new heroine?" he quipped.

"Isn't that the same thing?" Chelsie asked, although, in an instant, her analytical mind realized the difference. Brian, however, was already explaining.

"Not at all. Calling her Chelsie is simply a name for her. But making Chelsie your heroine means you will be the character."

"True. I realized the difference the moment I asked. Probably it will be the second!" she replied.

"Great." Brian grinned. "And am I going to be the protagonist?"

Chelsie didn't feel very comfortable answering him.

"No, his name is David."

"What's in a name?" Brian laughed, "So long as the character traits match."

"He's probably going to be a different kind of person," Chelsie said in a low voice.

Sitting at her desk the next day, she wondered why she'd reacted the way she did the evening before. Why wasn't she at ease discussing David with Brian? She'd always discussed her characters with him before embarking on the first draft. What was different this time?

Thinking about David gave her a clandestine pleasure. It was a kind of thrill she thought wasn't possible beyond the teenage years, and certainly not when someone had been married for six years.

Leaving the laptop open, she walked over to the window facing the woods and stared outside. A part of the lake could be seen but was better visible from their bedroom window. From there, they could even see the wooden jetty on this side of the lake. Was she discontented? Was she getting bored in her marriage?

Chelsie wasn't sure and knew that wasn't a good sign.

Day after day, she crafted David with care and affection. Day after day, she got herself entangled in his raw charm. She was attributing to him all the traits she imagined the men in her fantasies to possess. Only, they were nameless and often faceless – David had a name here. She had also started thinking of a face unlike anyone she knew. Not even the face of Michelangelo's David. No. His was too innocent. Her David would have a sensual glint in his eyes, yet serene enough to command love and respect. He'd be a person who would know exactly how to respond to every move Chelsie made when they came together. He would take cues from the twists or moans she made, and she wouldn't have to guide him constantly, as she had to do with Brian.

Chelsie forcibly aborted her train of thought the moment she thought of Brian.

She picked up the phone and called Amy.

"I'm in love," she blurted without warning as Amy answered.

Amy was taken aback. She knew Chelsie too well to believe she could be into something like that, but when Chelsie mentioned David, she understood. She had already heard.

"Go for him," she giggled. "It would be great to get screwed by that monster of his and out in the woods, too. Call me if you ever want a threesome." Amy couldn't stop chuckling.

But Chelsie wasn't laughing.

That evening, she changed her relationship status on Facebook from "Married" to "In a relationship."

CHAPTER 7

"So, who is this new love of yours?" Brian asked the next afternoon with a huge grin.

For a moment, Chelsie was caught off-guard. But then she realized what Brian was referring to. He had noticed her new Facebook status.

"It's David," she said, sounding as casual as possible.

Brian laughed for nearly a minute and said, "I'm proud of your dedication, honey! This is how it should be. Live your plot! It's the best thing you could do, like method acting, you know? Get under the skin of your characters, and your novel is bound to be a masterpiece."

Chelsie only smiled. But Brian's enthusiasm was hard to contain. He had learned most of her ideas centered around David over the past week. He believed that if executed well, this would be one character that would spill over from the novel's confines. It would be a complicated task; Chelsie had portrayed stereotypical characters for so long. But to come across as genuine, David must be handled with caution. Cross the line, and you will be venturing into bawdiness; stay within the limits and risk the confinements of formula romance.

"Which Chelsie posted the Facebook status?" he joked. "The character or author?"

"Who do you think?" Chelsie replied, evading a direct reply.

"Well, well, well! It all depends on how much you allow yourself to be captured in portraying your heroine. Either way, you'll have a great time with him."

"What does that mean?" she asked with some anxiousness.

"As the heroine's alter ego, you're going to have a virtual rendezvous with the virile rascal!" Brian started guffawing again. "Come to think of it," he continued. "I believe changing your relationship status was a great idea. It'll help you relate to your plot with greater intensity. Also, I think it's a clever marketing gimmick."

Chelsie said, "It's not a gimmick. I'm serious about the relationship. I'm in love with David."

"Indeed! You're his creator, so love him as Our Lord loves us all."

"I said, I'm serious," Chelsie replied with unexpected firmness. Brian looked deep into her eyes but didn't respond. He placed a comforting arm around her and felt Chelsie was stiff and protective. He gently pulled her down on the couch as a sudden surge of desire washed over him. For the first time in their married life, Chelsie refused to yield. Brian didn't break the embrace; Chelsie forced herself from it.

He didn't say anything but felt she must have been stressed out. Perhaps things were getting too much for her to handle, he thought with compassion.

****

It was a Sunday morning. Generally, Chelsie only wrote on Sundays if there were some pressing deadlines to complete. But today, she had gone back to her desk right after breakfast. Although unusual, Brian knew how immersed she was in the new plot and let her be. He went out for a walk, heading for the woods.

Summer had its own fragrance – especially in the forest. The warm, moist herbal aroma rose and fell as the breeze wafted, like notes in an orchestra conducted by some virtuoso. The dried and decaying leaves underneath, the flaming blossom overhead, and the woody barks around him conspired to drown his senses in a verdant symphony. Brian listened to the birds chirping, the chipmunks squeaking, and the wind whistling through the foliage.

He walked to the lake and settled on the grass. The dark depths seemed inviting. For him, the lakeside was the best place to be. He could sit there idly for hours on end and introspect. He felt blessed to have discovered a cottage amidst just the right surroundings. Here, he could be on his own – content and fulfilled – without bothering Chelsie, who was so immersed in her work.

Of course, he would have been delighted had Chelsie shown more interest in the outdoors. She was just not that type. Moreover, it took some serious effort on her part in the initial stages of a novel as she grappled with the plot, the characters, and the narrative. Brian thought of all the good times they'd had in their six years of marriage. It was like a dream. Recovering from his reveries, Brian hoped it didn't end like a dream – with a rude jolt.

Of course, he was sure she was in a temporary phase. And then he thought of David. He admired Chelsie's involvement in bringing her dream protagonist to life. Once complete, he'd surely be one unforgettable character. He couldn't help but smile while thinking of the robust masculinity Chelsie attributed to David. Brian compared his own dimension with David's, as jotted by Chelsie in her notes. He was a hunk, indeed! Definitely the stuff Chelsie's fantasies are composed of. Staring at the undulating shimmer created by the sun over the lake's surface, Brian thought of her fantasies. They'd been typical and restrained when they first met but turned bolder with time. Brian had always appreciated the unbridled eroticism she exuded; they turned him on in a big way. But that was entirely between the two of them. Now, going by the new novel's plot and the way David was unfurling, Brian felt their privacy was being laid bare to the public. He understood her desire to author a groundbreaking romance, yet – deep down – he doubted whether she was taking things too far.

In the evening, their conversation drifted to the new novel. They hardly talked of anything else nowadays. Brian mentioned striking the right balance between reality and fiction in books – particularly in a genre like romance – when Chelsie got worked up.

"Do you mean whatever I write is purely imaginary? Without a touch of reality anywhere?" she challenged Brian.

"That wasn't the point of our discussion," he replied cautiously.

"But that's what you're implying. I think every character I've ever developed comes straight from life. They're real!"

"Reality or factionalism is a precondition for fiction; I never meant that," said Brian defensively. "I want to emphasize balance."

"What kind of balance are you referring to?"

"A judicious mix of real and imaginary. Take David, for example. We both know he's a product of all your fantasies. Now, the fact that he's fashioned out of Chelsie Crammer's fantasies might enchant your readers and be used as a great marketing gimmick – but does it add anything to the book's literary value?"

Chelsie didn't reply. Brian, too, stopped short. He was treading on a raw nerve. The issue was delicate – and both knew it more than anyone else.

"So, what do you suggest?" Chelsie asked in a cold, impassive voice after a while.

"Write fiction and not a personal journal – that's for one! Letting lose all your fantasies on paper might not be the best strategy. At least, the critics would not let it pass."

"You think David is all fantasy?" Chelsie continued in the same cold voice.

"Come on!" Brian laughed. Even Chelsie felt somewhat relieved to see him laugh again. The situation had become too tense. However, she didn't let her guard down.

"Your David is a lovable brute chiseled out of your choicest erotic fantasies," Brian added, still grinning.

"Do you think there can't be someone like him in reality?" Chelsie asked.

"Perhaps yes, perhaps no; does it matter? The question is whether his characterization is realistic enough." Brian said casually.

"I think David is real, very real," Chelsie spoke with a firmness that surprised Brian.

"He's a real man," she added. "He's out there, and I love him."

The conviction in her voice made it difficult for Brian to respond. After a pause, he spoke again.

"Then what about me, honey?" He tried to make it sound casual and buoyant. "Are you no longer in love with me?"

"You don't understand," Chelsie replied with impatience. "You're a constant in my life, but David... well... he's an ideal, a destination a person like me would want to attain..."

Her words trailed off as Brian burst out in mirthful laughter. For the first time that evening, Chelsie laughed, too. It was challenging to ignore Brian's jovial side for long.

Dinner was spent making small talk. The atmosphere was expected as they talked about the flowering plants in their garden, the impending end of summer, Brian's school, and other trivia. After dinner, they watched TV for a while. And then Brian tried to nestle closer to his wife. Still watching TV, Chelsie didn't resist his advances initially. Encouraged, Brian cuddled and petted her like an enthusiastic teenager; he loved her voluptuous curves. He felt Chelsie's breath getting shallower and faster. Her body relaxed under his pleading touch.

"Let's go to bed," he whispered.

She didn't reply.

"Come on, let's go," he implored.

Her body stiffened.

He felt her erect nipples soften under his probing fingers. Her breathing was more prolonged now. They sat silently for a moment, his hands still awkwardly grasping her.

She said, "No!" with the finality of a verdict, rose from the couch, and walked towards her study.

****

It was late at night, and Chelsie was still seated at her desk in the study. She was tapping words intermittently on her laptop, stopping, thinking, and tapping again. Occasionally, she paused to think about how she had refused Brian after dinner. From the study, she had heard him go into the bedroom. He never fell asleep before her. Chelsie was sure he was still awake, reading.

Was she wrong in rejecting his advances? Chelsie was undecided. As she resumed typing, she heard a melodious tune playing on a harmonica somewhere. At first, she thought it was the TV. Perhaps he wasn't in the bedroom after all. But she realized the tune was coming from outside – not very far, but just below her window.

The melody was clear and lilting. Chelsie sat frozen at her desk. Who could it be at such an hour? The place was desolate. She turned with a start on hearing footsteps behind her. It was Brian. He, too, had heard it. Emboldened in Brian's presence, Chelsie rushed to the window and clicked open the latch.

The harmonica stopped playing. Hastily, she flung the window wide open and leaned over. Brian walked up behind her.

They could see no one in the dark.

CHAPTER 8

Brian was returning home from school when he met Bill.

"Holla!" cried the cheerful old man, flashing his cordial grin. He was carrying a basket of fruits similar to the one he'd given them the day he visited.

Brian smiled, and the two locked hands in a warm grasp.

"Was going your way," said Bill. "But now that we've met, I'll pass this on to you."

He held out the basket. "Here, grab it, son! It's for Chelsie. She loved them the other day, and I have a stockpile. You won't get them garden-fresh back in your city."

"Oh, thanks! But we're embarrassed," Brian said apologetically. "We don't grow anything, so this won't be a fair barter."

"Forget it!" waved Bill jauntily. "I'll only be too happy to serve your lady. Allow her some peace, and I'm sure she'll come up with another great book."

"I hope so, Bill. I appreciate your concern. But why don't you come with me and offer them to her in person?"

"I would…but you can act as an able courier." The old man tried to wave the topic into insignificance, and Brian didn't press him.

"Do visit us once in a while," he said.

"With all the old people leaving and the neighborhood getting lifeless, we must keep visiting one other. And I'd much appreciate it if you'd stop at my place whenever you like. I know your lady is occupied and has her novel to work on, but tell her a walk around the country and an occasional visit to an old neighbor might help remove the most stubborn writer's block."

They laughed aloud in unison. Taking leave from his elderly neighbor, Brian walked homeward in much lighter spirits. Of late, he'd been feeling uncharacteristically heavy-hearted.

He crossed the third elm tree and took the final turn leading to their cottage. It was a straight walk down the road to their gate from here. He could see the white house bordered with red bricks ahead. One could see their living room if the curtains were drawn aside from the large glass windows. Although the lights were not on inside, he could make out the couch and the mirror on the far end of the living room wall. There was already one mirror in their bedroom, and they debated the necessity of having a full-length mirror in the living room, too – but let it be.

As he flipped the latch and pushed the gate open, he discerned the form of a man standing in front of the mirror.

Brian stopped in his tracks – his right arm on the gate while the basket of fruit dangled from his left. He watched for a few uncertain moments and then stepped forward, clasping the latch behind him. Taking a couple of hesitant steps, he stopped and pondered. He wasn't sure why he behaved undecidedly, but his first thought wasn't to go straightaway for the entrance door. Instead, he was tempted to go around the porch toward the window that opened towards the forest and the lake.

As he tiptoed around the porch, Brian felt a vague sense of guilt enveloping his consciousness. It occurred to him that he was acting like a stranger in his own home for no apparent reason. Was he going to surprise someone? The stranger? Chelsie? Perhaps both? Or was there a chance he might be in for a big surprise? None of the possibilities comforted him.

He stopped at a short distance from the window. From here, the mirror was at a right angle so that he couldn't see the reflection. But he could very well see the intruder. Wearing a checkered full-sleeved shirt and a pair of blue denims, the well-built man stared at the mirror, changing posture occasionally. With the day waning and no lights on inside, the living room was shadowy, although it was clear enough for Brian to see the figure's movement. He watched in rapt attention as the person ran both arms against himself and caressed between his legs. He faced the mirror all the while. There was no one else inside.

Brian became concerned about Chelsie's wellbeing. Where was she? Emerging from his stupor, he cursed himself for being distracted and not rushing inside. Tearing away from the window, he headed for the door.

****

Chelsie had been writing all afternoon. She was finally getting the plot to make sense. It was beginning to get a contemporary feel, and the mix of description and anticipation seemed just right. In the plot, she'd introduced the female character –Chelsie as decided – and David was already communicating with her via social media. But David wasn't sure if the girl would respond positively to his advances. More importantly, he had yet not determined whether this girl was his type. Chelsie, the character, was in a different dilemma. She had suppressed her deepest desires for so long that she worried expressing them might make her seem abnormal to someone as sophisticated as David. Of course, she had yet to meet the man in person, but she could make out from their exchanges that he was a sensitive and passionate guy – and Chelsie was reluctant to repulse such a man so early in the relationship.

Chelsie, the author, paused and looked away from the laptop screen. Was she being too vague? Should she make David's true nature more obvious? If not, she feared David would resemble her previous urban protagonists. She needed to prevent that at all costs. But David must come across as a discerning person at the same time. That was the problem. Passion and discernment were strange bedfellows, and she was doubtful how to balance the two and still make David seem like a real-life character.

She needed to understand David with more perception. He was an alpha male – and Chelsie would make him look like one. But for that, she needed to get under his skin. She needed to slip into his shoes.

And then she remembered the trunk in the attic.

Feeling exhausted from reconstructing David, Chelsie decided she needed to refresh her mind. Since its initial discovery, she hadn't explored the trunk and thought it might be a good distraction.

Climbing the stairs to the attic, she rummaged through the clothes for some time when the idea struck her.

After careful consideration, she wore a checkered blue-and-green shirt and a pair of denims. Closing the lid of the trunk and about to descend from the attic, she thought of something else. She opened the top again, reached down deep inside, and, within a couple of seconds, came up with the olive briefs. Carrying the underwear and other clothing, she descended the attic and went to her study. She tossed the things on a chair and sat in front of her opened laptop, trying to think.

Supposing she was David, how would she woo the girl in question? How would David determine what kind of a person the girl was? Would he open up, or would he be content with dropping a hint or two in the most civil manner possible? Chelsie needed to know her inner psyche of David better. She needed to think like a man, so she put on the clothes to create the ambiance. Something prompted her to believe it would allow her to glimpse the persona of a man as virile as David.

Removing her clothes carelessly and revealing her sculpted figure in the dying light of the study, Chelsie eased herself inside the inviting folds of flannel and denim. Her tall, muscular frame filled them well – just like the last time. Pity, there was no mirror in the study. She walked to the living room and stood in front of the mirror. She looked wonderfully manly. For a better appreciation, Chelsie drew aside all the curtains to allow the dying daylight into the room. She ran her hands over her body with passion and interest. How would David react if he had access to such an eager body? And what would the girl do then? Chelsie tried to share her consciousness between the male and the female characters and felt a huge turn-on. Languidly, she dropped her hands between her legs.

A moment later, the doorknob turned, and Brian appeared at the door.

****

"What's this?" Brian asked.

It wasn't clear from his tone whether he was relieved or annoyed. It could have been both.

"What?" Chelsie queried back.

She was trying to sound casual, even frivolous.

"You're wearing them again?"

"Oh, come on, honey! I was trying them on."

"It's silly!" Brian sounded distinctly vexed.

"I needed to do some research," she explained. It sounded like a poor excuse, even to her ears.

"Research on men's clothes? I told you you might contract something from them. They must've been in the attic for a pretty long time."

"They're clean," Chelsie defended.

"Yet they might be unhygienic. And why wear them at all? What are you trying to find out?"

"Just how a man feels in them."

"Duh! You're acting foolish now. And you could've used my clothes…"

"No, I couldn't!" Chelsie cut him short. For the first time during the conversation, she sounded firm.

"And why not?"

"You know they don't fit me. I can't possibly get inside them."

Of course, Brian knew it but had forgotten in the heat of the argument.

Not knowing how to respond, Brian walked over to the dining table and put down the basket of fruits he'd been carrying. Both remained silent for a while. Then Brian said, "The basket is from Mr. Furlow. He was coming himself…"

Chelsie didn't reply.

Brian sat on the couch and gave her a long, hard look. She stood there, arms resting on her hips.

"What research?" he asked in a deliberate but calmer tone.

"I wanted to know how David would feel," Chelsie almost whispered. "How he would react in certain situations."

"But these aren't David's clothes, honey. This is throwaway stuff, and we need to do as much with them; throw them away!"

Did Chelsie shudder at the suggestion? Brian couldn't tell with certainty because dusk had rendered the indoors as blurred as the outdoors. No one bothered switching on the lights.

"I'm sorry, but these might be David's clothes." Chelsie's voice trembled through the gathering darkness. "I think they belong to him."

Brian let out a long sigh.

"I… was trying to feel what he would have felt."

Brian sat still.

"I needed to know how he would react to the girl!"

Brian said nothing.

"It was only for the novel." Now, she sounded distinctly apologetic.

Brian felt terrible and uncomfortable. He failed to understand how, and for what reason, his energetic and talented wife was transforming into a nervous and perhaps paranoid wreck.

"Please don't wear them," he said uneasily.

"I'll take them off," Chelsie said as if in a trance.

She got up and unbuttoned the shirt. Bundling it on the side of the couch, she reached for the zipper of the blue denim. Even in the darkened room, Brian could see she wasn't wearing a bra or camisole. That wasn't unusual, but as the denim went down, he stared wide-eyed at the olive briefs clinging to her shapely bottom.

Without removing them, Chelsie picked up the shirt and the denim and walked toward her study.

****

It was an uneasy night for the couple. Chelsie didn't work late and went to bed right after dinner. Brian didn't indulge in his customary bedtime reading and switched off the lights early. But neither fell asleep, and each knew the other was awake, although both tried to make every toss and turn as stealthily as possible.

Outside, the night was calm. Occasional calls of cicadas coming from the forest accentuated the stillness. Summer was at its peak, and the weather was warm, although a breeze blowing across the lake kept the cottage comfortably cool.

Lying there on the bed, staring into the darkness, Chelsie and Brian heard the harmonica together. It played the same tune as the other night – evocative of melodies from Bohemia, simultaneously playful and reflective. But this time, it wasn't as close as before.

No one moved momentarily, and then Chelsie sat on the bed. As she reached for the switch, Brian resisted her.

"No lights!" he whispered.

Then he jumped out of bed and ran towards the window on nimble feet. Chelsie followed close behind.

Brian opened the window overlooking the lake. Chelsie realized why Brian had stopped her from switching on the light. The lake was visible from their bedroom. The full moon's light shimmered on the water and the treetops in the forest just beyond the lake. In the silver and blue illumination, they distinctly saw the silhouette of a man standing on the wooden jetty by the side of the lake. Tall and well-built, he was leaning against the guard rail – his head and arms motion indicated he was playing a harmonica. He was about a hundred meters away, and seeing his face was impossible. Brian knew it was pointless to give chase. He'd disappear inside the forest beyond the lake when the guy saw him approaching.

They stood transfixed at the window as the soulful tune filled the night air.

CHAPTER 9

Chelsie made deliberate alterations to her routine for the last couple of days. She started work early, much before breakfast – even before Brian got out of bed. The new schedule was in total contrast to her lifelong pattern of work. For the first few days, she felt groggy in the morning. Not that she got less sleep, but now she went to bed after dinner.

The abrupt lifestyle change bothered Brian initially. Although Chelsie hadn't offered a direct explanation, he eventually linked her transformation to the two episodes of ghostly serenade. But that wasn't the sole reason. Chelsie felt awkward with Brian after the night they had argued over the attic clothes. It was easier for her to head to bed right after dinner without spending time together in front of the TV or making small talk. She also felt uneasy when Brian waited for her to come to bed after working late. True, he did his reading then – but it was a waiting Chelsie tried to avoid. Getting up sooner compensated for the time she lost at night and allowed her to evade morning conversations.

Brian had stopped reading in bed, fearing the light might disturb her. He now read in the study after dinner. It was a complete role reversal. Only Brian would have stayed awake in bed most nights, waiting for her to finish work and join him; Chelsie, on the other hand, invited sleep as a refuge.

The spooky serenade had affected their mental well-being – there was no doubt about that. They weren't afraid because the man hadn't done anything intimidating. Chelsie doubted whether he had even done anything illegal. The lake and the forest were public property; anyone could play the harmonica there. Brian wasn't sure whether the first serenade was performed right below her study window. If so, that meant the person was trespassing on their property. But they hadn't seen him and couldn't prove anything. Chelsie wasn't sure whether the man was serenading them – or her. There was nothing except the lilting tune to give away the man's intentions; however soulful it was, it was without words.

The incident remained stuck in their minds, like a sore that wasn't painful but bothersome nonetheless.

However, Chelsie had made good progress with the novel since she started experimenting with the attic clothes. She tried them on during the day when Brian was away, which felt remarkably liberating. The clothes seemed to enclose her with a warmth that, over time, became addictive. She felt her tender skin communicate with the fabric, and her body opened to unexplored possibilities. She could think of things – new themes, new fantasies, and unique courses of action – that helped her navigate the plot effortlessly.

She was guiding her character, Chelsie, to take bold steps. The girl had had enough of beating around the bush and was curious to explore the other side of David. She suspected David was eager to share secrets, and she was ready to play along. However, she wanted him to make the first move – and that was where Chelsie, the author, had gotten stuck. She needed her heroine to drop subtle hints to David so he knew she was the girl for him. Alternatively, she could make David drop hints for the girl, but that might not go down well with loyal readers accustomed to the formula of having the guy make the first move.

Chelsie was wary that the dilemma might cause her to lapse into her familiar pattern. No, she would steer the plot differently, but simultaneously, she wanted David to take the first step. It would be natural and graceful if he came out of his self-imposed cocoon and acted macho. She wanted him to cast aside gentleness and reveal raw sexuality sooner. She expected him to lead Chelsie into throes of passion.

Chelsie the character or Chelsie the author? She wasn't sure about that one.

****

One morning, while taking sluggish sips from her coffee mug to drive away an overnight lethargy, Chelsie turned on the laptop and scrolled until she reached where she had left off the evening before. Surprisingly, she couldn't place the last sentence. She glanced up and then scrolled through the text. The events appeared unfamiliar. She read more closely. The dialogue was fresh, and it was her style, without a doubt. The casual brilliance, the warmth, and the spark of passion stood intact, yet the events were unfamiliar.

Chelsie's manicured fingers flicked impatiently over the gray touchpad. Finally, she located where she'd stopped the previous evening. It was a good seven pages above the end of the text.

Perplexed, she read through the new addition to the draft. It opened with a chapter where David was thinking of Chelsie in some detail. They had yet to meet but shared photos. David was thinking of everything they'd shared over social media. How he analyzed it showed that the girl had already laid her heart bare, although unintentionally. David was an expert in the game of love and quickly realized this was his girl. He was sure she had the perfect balance of warmth and kink he'd always fantasized about but had never known in a person.

Chelsie read with suspended breath. She had prepared the ground for this analysis through everything she'd drafted about the girl. Yet she had never looked at things the way David did. It was apparent he had read all the clues the character Chelsie had given during online conversations.

Her heart missed a beat as she approached the end of the newly appended text.

David had proposed to meet Chelsie for a cup of coffee. He intended to ask her out for a date that weekend.

As she read the lines, Chelsie was transported to her teens, when every request for a date seemed a gateway to unknown bliss. She didn't notice when Brian walked in and sat on the couch by the window. When she did, she blushed and locked the laptop screen in one swift motion.

She finished her coffee, which had turned cold by then. Turning towards Brian, she announced calmly, "I told you David was real."

Brian turned from the window in surprise.

"Someone has added seven pages to my manuscript!"

"What do you mean?"

"Yesterday, I left off on page forty-nine, and today, I find the draft ends on page fifty-six."

"Check the line spacing or the font," Brian said casually. "Sounds like a formatting issue."

"They're perfectly all right."

"Look at the margins then, or even random page breaks. Look for blank pages."

"I've checked everything!" Chelsie retorted with some irritation. "What do you think I am?"

"Was only trying to help you, honey." Brian grinned.

"I'm sorry." Chelsie toned down. "But look here! Seven pages of new text seem to have been written by me. Yet, I swear I never thought of this sequence. Although I must admit, it has helped me overcome a tight spot in the narrative."

"This change in your daily routine will take some time to get used to." Brian smiled again. "Your body clock is failing to keep up with the sudden alteration. You're sleep-deprived, that's all."

"What has that got to do with this?"

"You must have dozed off last evening while working. Then you tried to push yourself ahead, slipping in and out of slumber. That last chapter must have been composed in a transcendental state. It happens."

Chelsie fell silent. That has happened. However, she always remembers where she ends the final train of thought in such cases. And this time, she distinctly remembers closing the document and shutting down the laptop. She even remembers walking over to the window after that. She was perfectly awake, no doubt about it.

Amy called that afternoon. They chatted aimlessly for a while.

Chelsie said, "David asked me out on a date."

"Who?" Amy was confused for a moment. Then she remembered. "Oh, your country bumpkin?"

"My hero. And let me remind you, David is no bumpkin. He knows French and Latin, plays the violin, is an expert in martial arts, and is extremely sensitive to women's feelings."

"He's also a great lay!" Amy giggled.

"Anyway, he is opening up now, and that's the most important thing. Let me see what happens on our date this weekend." Chelsie sounded serious.

Amy was much amused. As she hung up, she couldn't help but admire the creative instincts of her dear friend.

****

The date went off like a dream. Chelsie put her best efforts into that sequence on Sunday night but was tentative in scripting David's actions and was conservative in her approach.

She was in for a sweet surprise when she opened the laptop on Monday morning.

Two new chapters had been added overnight. Several alterations had been made to the dating sequence. The changes resulted in a bolder and stronger David, who spoke with charm and was more direct in his approach than Chelsie had initially written. David sends a long e-mail to Chelsie after the date in one of the new chapters. In it, he exposes his darkest desires to her for the first time in terms that set Chelsie, the author, on fire. In the other chapter, David and Chelsie engage in a revealing phone call that can only lead to one thing – passionate and explosive, yet tremulous with an undertone of sweet sensuality.

After reading the added scene, Chelsie was even more convinced David was real and communicating with her through the manuscript. Although she knew it defied reason, no other explanation could account for the strange occurrence.

Day after day, it went on. She would write several pages and wake up the next morning to find new scenes added to the manuscript. The additions fashioned David into a man of flesh and blood. Executed beautifully, he was turning out to be the most significant character Chelsie ever created. She called Amy and Linda and gushed about how David was more of a man than Brian. She talked about David in absolute terms, and her friends laughed but warned her not to strain herself in writing. They suspected she was stressed because she sounded on a constant high during their conversations.

Brian was initially concerned that Chelsie had suffered from hallucinations. He tried to talk her out of believing the manuscript was being written by itself – or, more importantly, by David. However, most conversations started to end in heated and one-sided arguments. So, he stopped discussing the topic altogether and no longer interfered with his wife's fantasy.

He missed her in bed, as well as in his daily routine. They no longer took long walks together in the afternoon either.

CHAPTER 10

Chelsie opened the door to find Bill standing outside with a guilty smile.

"What a pleasant surprise!" she exclaimed. "Please come in."

Bill entered and held out his hand. He was clasping a bunch of yellow roses. It wasn't professionally arranged, but an assortment of freshly picked flowers gathered in a bouquet. A few leaves still cling to some of the stems.

"A small present from my garden," he said shyly.

"It's wonderful. And so were the fruits you sent the other day."

She took the roses, inhaled deeply, and said, "It looks like your garden has everything... fruits, flowers.... I'd so like to visit it."

"My invitation doesn't have a 'best before' date." Bill smiled. "You are always welcome. A visit from you is long overdue. That's what I told your husband when we met last. Where is he, by the way?"

"Gone for a walk by the lake. It's where he usually spends most of his Sunday mornings, either there or in the woods."

"He loves nature, I can understand that. It's a good thing. Mark my words, young lady, fifty years from now, we will regret not having spent enough outside. The way we maltreat nature, it won't be there long."

Chelsie loved the passionate way the elderly gentleman uttered his conviction. To her, as well as to Brian, Bill resembled the best America had to offer. He epitomized the old-fashioned essence of the American way of life.

Unable to match his enthusiasm, Chelsie said, "Brian loves it here, especially the lake."

And then she remembered something.

"Do you know of anyone who plays the harmonica around here?"

"The harmonica?" Bill thought hard but shook his head. "No one I can think of. Why do you ask?"

Chelsie decided not to elaborate. Nothing had happened, really. She shook her head casually and said, "I was just wondering. We thought we heard someone playing one."

"Don't know. The old fellow Simon used to play the violin. But he has been lying under the ground for over a decade."

"It's all right; it must be a mistake."

Just then, Brian returned and was happy to see Bill. The two exchanged greetings and started conversing about the types of trees in the local forest. They talked while Chelsie listened silently, wondering whether she should excuse herself. Bill could tell things weren't the same between the couple. They avoided eye contact, and Brian was more reluctant and subdued. As he left, he decided to visit them more often. Chelsie, too, promised they would see Bill's cottage soon.

Bill began visiting at regular intervals. He was especially mindful of Chelsie. He always brought small gifts for her and displayed innumerable signs of affection and care. Chelsie wasn't sure if there was a reason or whether it was just his loving nature.

During one of his visits, Bill asked, "Have you been to the small town beyond the town?"

"No," she shook her head.

"Neither have I," said Brian. "But I've been planning to go ever since we arrived."

"Go this weekend and take her along." Bill pointed at Chelsie. "They're holding the annual county fair this time of year. It would be an experience for you. And it would be a good opportunity to learn more about the rural way of life."

Brian said at the dinner table that evening, "Would you care to visit the fair this weekend?"

"Not a bad idea," Chelsie replied, not sounding too enthusiastic.

"It will help you gather insight on local life."

"That's what I hope," she said.

"So it's final then? We'll go this Saturday. It would be great if we walked – although it's quite a distance if we go through town. We can take a shortcut instead."

"A long walk?" Chelsie's query carried no emotion.

"No, not if we take the detour. We'll avoid town altogether, get to the lake, and then turn north, leaving the forest track to our right. From there, it's a quarter of a mile until the town church on the southern fringes. We turn right beyond the church, and it's another quarter mile from there."

"Have you gone before?" Chelsie knew he hadn't yet and was slightly surprised to hear such precise directions.

"No, I've walked beyond the church on this route, but no further. The rest I learned from others at school."

"Okay, let's go," said Chelsie.

"You and I!" Brian flashed his warm smile.

This time, Chelsie smiled, too.

****

Quaint and vintage, it looked like time stood still at the fair. Music, food, farm animals and livestock, jugglers, exhibits, rides, and roller coasters – all woven together in a tapestry of noise and color, an unending jamboree of life. Upon entering the fairgrounds, Brian stopped in his tracks and took in the grand sight – a perfect scene that evoked popular Art Deco posters from the early twentieth century. The fairs he remembered as a child were stinky, mainly because there were too many animals. Now, although animals were there, the predominant aroma was food. The air was laden with the smell of grilled corn, well-seasoned with butter and garlic salt. There were a variety of sandwiches, and each looked healthy and edible. Brian bought and ate a cream donut as he wandered through the carnival crowd.

Chelsie didn't feel like eating so soon. She wanted to check out the wares displayed in the stalls. They mainly were household gadgets like slicers, dicers, cleaners, peelers, and choppers. There were decorative trinkets for every conceivable part of the human anatomy, and teenagers thronged those booths. There were several photo and craft exhibits, a school art show, and a talent show where locals displayed their abilities on a raised platform.

And then there were the contests. They had day-long tractor races featuring different classes, including functional antique models. There was the Favorite Pie Cooking Contest, the Potato Decorating Contest, and even a Great Pumpkin Contest, further divided into several categories: animal shapes, the funniest and scariest pumpkins, most unique shape, and a few others. Brian was especially amused by the plethora of farm exhibits prefixed with superlatives: super pigs, wonder bulls, sturdy horses, intelligent dogs, and awesome blossoms! As they strolled past neat rows of magnum-sized cabbages and cauliflowers, Chelsie bought some cotton candy and tentatively picked at it.

They headed home as the sun went beyond the Ferris wheel and dipped below the circus tent. The day had been warm, but it gradually cooled as they left the fair and approached the forest road. Brian wore the carnival hat he had bought, and Chelsie carried the knickknacks she'd collected. The din of the fair faded behind them as daylight waned. They walked – neither close nor far apart –lost in a personal labyrinth of thoughts.

Brian was thinking of his dad, who he'd lost while still a boy. His earliest memories of fairs were associated with his dad, a mirthful man who enjoyed social gatherings. His grandfather had a farm, and during summer vacations, his dad made it a point to take Brian. "You need to know nature, up, close and personal," he would say. "Civilization sprang from nature and not the other way round. Never stray too far from your origins, or finding your way back will become too difficult."

Brian still fondly remembered his vacations at the farm. And, of course, his dad took him to all the nearby county fairs. He used to say he loved a fair's noise, smell, and pulsating bustle. Today, Brian realized what his dad had meant for the first time.

Chelsie wondered how cotton candy's taste had remained the same for over three decades. She hadn't been a regular visitor to fairs in her childhood. Her mother had dust allergies, and her father was too busy in his professional life to care for juvenile distractions. However, her little memory of the few fairs she'd visited was predominantly of cotton candy – its taste and aroma.

Her father never spent much time with her. He was a successful physician and only cared about Chelsie's grades. She was intelligent and never disappointed him, but she'd been lonely. It was the primary reason she'd read books very early. She was a voracious reader; it was how she'd come to know the world. Yet, she always wished her dad would play with her, read to her, or spend weekends at home. It never happened.

It was dark and blustery, and the wind whistled through the woods when they reached the lake. Moments later, they heard the harmonica.

It played the same old tune. By now, Chelsie could have hummed along with it – it had become so familiar. Brian stopped and turned towards the woods.

"Let's get home," Chelsie murmured.

"Just trying to see if there's any light in the forest," Brian whispered.

"Get going," she insisted.

The tune continued in the background as they hurried along the shores of the lake. The cool bridge sent a shiver down her spine as Chelsie strode in haste.

CHAPTER 11

Was it David serenading her? Chelsie couldn't help but believe it. She knew he could play the violin and attributed that quality to him. There was no harm in adding the harmonica to his Curriculum Vitae; he played so well. Although she had been nervous hearing it that evening, she secretly hoped he played a different tune next time. While each episode made her uneasy, now she wanted a next time. She would like to hear all the songs David knew. The almost surreal image of the man standing on the old jetty awash in blue and silver moonlight kept haunting her. He'd been tall, had broad shoulders, and played with a casual grace only a true hero from a Chelsie Crammer Romance could have done. David was her most fabulous character ever: the most heroic, the most sophisticated, and, at the same time, the most virile. When Brian had stopped and peered into the forest, Chelsie's heart had skipped a beat. She expected the man to appear at any moment. Paradoxically, she did and didn't want it to happen and had urged Brian to move on.

Brian was a little shaken since that evening. For the first time, he felt they were being stalked. Because the cottage was desolate and he spent most of the day at school, he was concerned about Chelsie's safety. He contemplated quitting his teaching job but knew it wasn't a solution. Moreover, given the level of understanding – or the lack of it – in their relationship, teaching gave him some relief, and he felt his new job also gave him a new perspective on life.

"Do you think we should call the cops?" he asked Chelsie the next day.

"Regarding what?" Chelsie was thinking of something else.

"Regarding the harmonica affair. I have a feeling we're being stalked."

Stalked! Chelsie felt the cold shiver down her spine that evening in the woods return. Someone was stalking them… stalking her! A tall and broad-shouldered man whose lips must be as graceful on other lips as on a harmonica. She tried to conceal a blush and remain casual. She felt like a nineteen-year-old.

"Do you think so?" she said.

Brian became a little impatient. "What else do you think he's doing in the woods? There's no one else around other than us!"

"But that might be precisely why he comes here to play the harmonica; it's secluded."

Brian paused and reflected on the unexpected reasoning. For a moment, he wasn't sure whose safety he was concerned about.

"Look, honey," he argued. "It's lonely here, and I stay away almost all day. Wouldn't it be prudent to keep the cops informed?"

"We'll look silly jumping the gun! The cops can always be called if there is a genuine emergency. In any case, they can't do anything about it right now."

Her logic being perfect, Brian didn't press further, but he was very disturbed on the inside. Over and above the suspense regarding the harmonica, his wife's nonchalant attitude snowballed into a new source of concern.

The following day, Brian met Bill on his way to school. He thought it best not to share details regarding the serenade below their study window or that they had seen someone by the lake. Instead, he summarized by saying someone was playing the harmonica at night by their cottage and asked Bill if he knew anything about it.

"Your wife asked me the same thing the last time I visited," Bill said. "I have no clue what is going on."

"Do you know anyone at all who plays the harmonica?" Brian asked.

"I can't think of anyone," replied a perplexed Bill.

****

Seated at her desk, Chelsie was unable to concentrate on her writing. No new chapters had been added for the last few days, and the novel seemed stuck. She wasn't in the right frame of mind to execute something creative. It would have been an immense help had her unknown co-author intervened.

Unknown co-author! She dwelt on the term with some indulgence. For all she knew, it was David. For the pure and simple reason, it must have been that it couldn't be anyone else. But was the harmonica player David as well? Or a stalker, as Brian suggested? The term 'stalker' was assuming a menacing connotation in her mind. Yes, she might be in danger… threatened perhaps…if the harmonica player wasn't David. Chelsie believed she would have felt much safer with David coming home through the woods that evening. David was the guy to be with on such occasions, not Brian.

The thought got her creative juices flowing, and she enthusiastically tapped on the laptop. She was going to introduce an episode in the novel where her character, Chelsie, was stalked by a stranger while on a second date with David. They had driven to some secluded spot to enjoy the sunset. David wanted to explore the area on foot as the sun went down, and they strolled around for some time. It was then the stranger intercepted.

Chelsie left the episode unfinished on purpose, anticipating David would complete it. His response would reveal how he would have dealt with the harmonica player had he been the one accompanying her that evening.

David responded as expected. The following day, she found the unfinished episode neatly typed in language that always read in sync with hers.

Chelsie eagerly scanned the chapter. Yes! David had acted like the man he was, a true debonair. He had boldly confronted the stranger and challenged his motives. Not satisfied with whatever the man mumbled, he had given him a shove. When the man had sprung open a two-fold knife and advanced menacingly for a counterattack, David used his advanced knowledge of hand-to-hand combat to fight back adroitly and, in just two nimble and well-poised strikes, brought the man to his knees – his knife flung away in the darkness of the surrounding foliage. As Chelsie the character watched in awe and Chelsie the author read with equal admiration, David – his thunderous sinews bulging – hauled the person up by the scruff of his neck and gave him one final punch to conclude the encounter. Chelsie was almost compelled to applaud his grand show of chivalry and might as she read.

But that wasn't the end of it. Leaving the hopeless stalker a complete wreck, David casually asked Chelsie to complete their idyllic walk down the forest track.

Chelsie said, "It's dark."

David replied, "What else do you expect after the sun goes down?"

"Let's go back," Chelsie murmured.

"Scared of the dark, are you?" David queried.

"Get going," she insisted.

"Come on, it never gets that dark out in the open. Besides, that guy is down and out."

"There might be other outlaws hanging around here in the wild."

"Even if there were, what could they do?" David gave her a killer smile that glowed, even in the dark.

"It's terrible!" Chelsie said as she grabbed David's arm.

"Not with me around," David said with a calm confidence that exuded strength and dependability. Chelsie felt a sense of security wrapping her up like a warm blanket. Holding his arm tightly, she was led into the woods.

Reading this far, Chelsie looked up and away from her laptop. "What's going to happen next? Why is David leading me inside the forest? Is it going to be the climax of the novel? Are we going to get physical?" Chelsie asked herself.

Chelsie knew it was perilous to portray an entire sexual encounter too early in the plot. If you had to, introducing some new crisis would require keeping the narrative going and sustaining the reader's interest. A safer, tried, and tested formula was to put off the final explosive union towards the end of the novel, after which nothing much was expected apart from tying up loose strings and having the main characters settle into a life of happily ever after. This was a blueprint for success, and no romance lover worth her salt would ever turn the final page with dissatisfaction after reading this. Chelsie knew she could easily pull off the winning formula yet again, but she wanted a different book to satisfy her existing fans and win her new ones. She was curious about what her co-author had in mind, so she resumed reading.

Sure enough, David was seducing Chelsie in the woods. Of course, he was neither blunt nor gross, and his dapper charm made every advance seem like a dream for both Chelsies. He clarified to Chelsie that he was interested in revealing his deepest passions, provided she played along and revealed her own secrets. It was to celebrate eroticism based on deep mutual trust and reciprocal spontaneity, a meeting of two like-minded people looking for the perfect soul mate.

David made it clear that willingness was a prerequisite in this game. He would certainly not impose himself because, to him, this wasn't a one-night stand or a fling; he'd had enough of those. What he sought was someone he could explore sexual blessings with. It was more than sex – it was a commitment towards ideal companionship.

David rested his case in no uncertain terms, and now it was up to Chelsie to respond. She realized David could be the answer to her dreams, but she feared he might not be serious enough. And what if he was repulsed once she revealed her wild side? What would she do?

What would Chelsie, the author do? Her co-author had taken the plot to a point of no return. From here, she would have to make a call. She tried to recreate the situation in her mind and evoke the emotions involved. There she was, with David in the lonely woods, her stalker vanquished and her hero exuding confidence. She was clutching his manly arm – so unlike Brian's – brawny and hairy. The warm aroma of the summer forest, his strong masculine odor, and fresh cologne made a heady mix; what lady could ignore that? She would have accepted the invitation to carnal bliss, as would thousands of her teenage readers. Chelsie realized well enough that the plot could only head towards denouement after the union. In that case, the story would remain a simple narrative of finding Mr. Right, with no added dimension or credentials to claim itself as the Great American Novel!

But what a sweet submission it would be! Chelsie envied her heroine and longed to meet David, the epitome of the ideal male. Oh, how she would give up everything to get physical with David! A flame of passion seared through her body. It twirled around her breasts, danced over her belly, and scorched her loins. She twitched, turned in her chair, and realized she had never encountered a total and complete sexual experience. What she once thought was bliss was nothing but child's play. And what she'd considered fulfillment was sheer compromise. Yes, compromises.

She was one of the most successful bestselling authors ever in the American Pacific Northwest, intelligent, witty, beautiful, and lusty. With passion, very few women could match – why should she compromise? Why shouldn't the world grovel at her feet? Or, more importantly, why should she not be wooed by a Superman like David? She deserved him as much as he deserved her. The thoughts drove Chelsie into a frenzied state. She was sure he was going to be her erotic match.

The doorbell jolted her out of her agitated reverie. It was still too early in the afternoon for Brian to return, and Bill only visited in the mornings. Was it the stalker? Or David?

Unable to contain herself, Chelsie rushed out of the study and flew to the door, crying in a playful tone, "I'm coming, darling!"

A pleasantly surprised Brian, flashing his trademark grin, jolted Chelsie out of her reverie for the second time that afternoon.

"School got out early today," he said as he entered.

A succession of emotions paraded through Chelsie's mind. But all she finally said was, "I was writing!"

Then she hurried back to her desk. The afternoon was marred, and she cursed Brian silently. She hated him.

What was she doing in that God-forsaken cottage? It was no life! She wanted a life; she wanted David.

****

Brian ate some cereal and then contemplated what to do for the afternoon. It was apparent Chelsie was preoccupied with her writing, so he decided to go for a walk by himself.

Summer days had progressed towards mellow fruitfulness. The aroma of blooming hazelnuts hung heavy in the air. Sparrows gathered on the fence fluttered away as Brian swung open the gate and walked out. Since he began teaching, Brian usually only went for weekend afternoon walks. Today was a refreshing change. He inhaled the fragrance of maturing summer and strolled towards the lake.

Each treetop was abuzz with activity. The birds scoured for food all day, and now fledglings demanded their share. With their little beaks wide, exposing tender red mouths eagerly awaiting morsels of food, the young ones sang a chorus that filled the air. Soon, pangs of hunger will be satiated. The woods would be silent, and Brian would return to the cottage.

Sitting by the side of the lake, Brian reflected. Although he seldom expressed personal frustrations, he was disappointed that the visit to the fair failed to revive their relationship. Plotting a togetherness graph, he shuddered about how their relationship had plummeted since moving to the countryside. They were a perfect couple – both in body and in soul. But what was supposed to be an idyllic country vacation was the grave of their marriage. Was the area to blame? Or was it the cottage? Who was the harmonica player stalking them? And why was Chelsie getting so worked up with the plot of her new novel? Why did she believe David had been writing her novel each night? Was it creative imagination or psychotic hallucination? He felt it was time to intervene.

And yet he loved this place. After the urban rush, he found a cosmic harmony, his own pace of life close to nature, and then there was the lake. Brian stared at its calm waters with a fond gaze.

****

They had their worst fight ever that night at the dinner table.

Chelsie had been lost in her thoughts, but Brian was determined to broach the topic of her changed behavior. The moment he mentioned it, she flared up.

"I've come to this place with a plan to complete the best novel of my career. This isn't a honeymoon, so don't expect me to accompany you on every little jungle safari!"

"That wasn't my point," Brian tried to keep calm. "Everyone respects your work, including me. It's just that you are going overboard with your novel."

"What do you mean?" Chelsie almost screamed.

"Look, you're talented enough to write a novel, but how you imagine things…"

He couldn't finish. Chelsie screamed at the top of her lungs, "I'm not imagining!"

Brian just looked at her. Nostrils flared and eyes rolling, she shouted again, "I'm not imagining one little thing. Everything's true! Everything's real! All the characters are based on real life."

This time, Brian lost his composure.

"Grow up, Chelsie!" he rebuked her sternly. "You're too clever to act like a neurotic fool. An author of your stature must keep fantasy and imagination apart."

"David is real – if that's what you're hinting at. He's real, he's out there, and he's waiting for me! Even his clothes are up in the attic. He's more real than our boring relationship, more alive, and much more of a man than you!"

"You're mad!" he shouted. "Stop this nonsense."

Chelsie shoved her unfinished plate and sprang from her chair. The chair tumbled backward and landed with a thud as the plate glided past Brian, dropped over the table's edge, and exploded in a hundred shards all over the floor.

CHAPTER 12

"I'm sorry!" Chelsie said to Brian the following day.

He smiled but said nothing.

"I'm sorry for my behavior, but I still say David is real," Chelsie said with conviction. "I just need to find out how he's getting access to my laptop," she continued. "Not that I mind, but it's spooky. It would have helped had we known what kind of people lived in this house before we moved in."

"The agent said the house was unoccupied for quite some time," Brian spoke softly and uncharacteristically detachedly.

"But it had been occupied before that."

"I think so."

"So it seems, from the trunk in the attic," Chelsie murmured.

After Brian left for school, Chelsie settled at her desk. The confrontation with Brian the night before had been cathartic for her to some extent. After days of pent-up frustration, it felt good to release it. And she was happy to declare that her husband was no match for David. It cleared up a lot of confusion and false expectations, and she'd at least be able to maintain a working relationship with Brian without the awkwardness and acting evasive.

As she scrolled through the manuscript, she reasoned with herself. Her co-author hadn't added anything since the episode in the forest ended with David's invitation, and now it was Chelsie's turn to respond. However temperamental and fanciful she might be, Chelsie was true to her art. She had correctly decided not to let her heroine yield to the temptations, and no, the time had not yet come. She wanted to build up the tension further. Let her readers simmer in anticipation; the final release would be mind-blowing! This romance would seize the nation's fancy like no one had before. It was her forte, and she thought it fair enough to aim at a Pan-American readership through romance and not another genre. Let them judge if Chelsie Crammer was not a real author. Even D. H. Lawrence had produced an affair with Lady Chatterley, despite all annotations and footnotes academicians might have added to that novel.

So, that was it. Chelsie had not yielded to David in the woods, and he had accepted her decision. The plot has taken a couple of new bends, and Chelsie is gradually paving the way for the grand climax. As she crafted the story, she waited for a culminating sexual release. She was certain David would respond, and then, one day, they would meet for the ultimate rendezvous.

But was she daydreaming? She understood well enough that the way her novel was getting written was weird, yet wonderful. Her friends didn't believe Brian was trashing the idea; she knew it was bizarre. She should be terrified of the whole thing and questioning the security of the cottage or thinking of getting medical help. But her mind was lucid, and the work of her co-author was right there on her laptop monitor. How could she not believe it was real?

She thought learning more about the previous occupants was a good idea.

Brian, too, contemplated throughout the day. He was thinking of the harmonica player. Was he targeting them, or did he have something to do with the past cottage owners? After school, Brian met the pastor of the town church. He was amiable, and Brian hoped he would know everyone around. The pastor had only been there for about four years, and the cottage had been unoccupied. Nevertheless, he could identify the cottage well enough because of its location.

"It's a nice cottage, and I much appreciate the solitude, but it stood mostly neglected."

Then he remembered something. "Emily told me once that she used to work as a maid there," he blurted.

"Who's Emily?" asked a surprised Brian.

"A woman from town. Her mother, Louisa, is a devout lady. Up until last year, she visited the church regularly. I hear she's too old for that now. I've not seen Emily for a while, but the last time I heard from her, she was looking for a job."

"We can find them in town, then?" Brian enquired.

"You should be able to. Just ask anyone, and they'll show you where Louisa Fenton lives. She's quite a popular figure. Just be forewarned; she talks a lot!"

Brian smiled. "We want to listen, so that won't be much of a problem."

"Don't say I didn't warn you!" laughed the pastor.

That evening, Brian told Chelsie everything the pastor had told her.

"I'll go meet with Emily," she said.

"I can come, too, if you go over the weekend." Brian proposed.

"Let's wait and see," Chelsie replied absentmindedly. She wasn't too keen to go with Brian.

****

After Brian left for work the next day, she decided to go to town alone. She finished an early lunch and then took the best-fitting checkered shirt from the trunk in the attic and paired it up with her blue jeans. She no longer felt guilty wearing the clothes, nor did she think it necessary to conceal the fact from Brian if he found out.

Initially, she thought of taking the road through town but changed her mind once she was outdoors. Instead, she took the shortcut they'd taken to the county fair. She went beyond the lake and turned north by the fringes of the forest. The blue sky was interspersed with sun and clouds, and a strong breeze made for pleasant weather. Soon, the church steeple came into sight. Another fifteen minutes and she was in town.

The first person she met promptly gave her directions to Louisa Fenton's house. It was a modest home in good condition. As Chelsie approached the front walk, two neighborhood children ran ahead and announced her arrival.

"Grandma, you've got a guest!" they shouted from the porch as they thumped on the door.

A well-rounded old lady unfastened the door and peered out. She squinted to adjust to the bright daylight and finally rested her gaze on Chelsie.

"Good morning!" Chelsie smiled. "I'd like to meet Emily... your daughter."

"Emily," muttered the old lady. "Emily... why, she's gone away to New Orleans."

"New Orleans?" Chelsie's voice didn't hide her disappointment.

"Yes! But do come in, missus!" exclaimed Mrs. Fenton. "Where did you come from?"

"Beyond the town near the woods; I stay in one of the cottages over there."

"Oh, the cottages. Great place, nice lake, good people...come inside, please." As she moved sideways, Chelsie stepped in.

"Will your daughter be gone for long?" she asked.

"She came last Christmas; God only knows when she'll come next! It's a good job she secured there. We talked to Mr. Jenson at the post office, and he said New Orleans would be great for her, and she has secured work as a maid for a wealthy family. She will have opportunities to learn things in a big household. The Coopers are big people. During her Christmas visit, she said they were good to her, and she hoped for a raise this July. Lord knows the hardships our family has been through, and now we're getting what we rightfully deserve. We hadn't had a moment's peace since her father died over half a century ago. But I always told my children to stay firm and committed, and the world would give you what you deserve."

Chelsie wondered how old the lady was and what age Emily would be if her father had died fifty years ago! As Louisa Fenton paused to catch her breath, Chelsie hastened to say, "I thought Emily could give me some information about the occupants of one of the cottages."

"Ask me, good lady, I know each of them. The Gables was the first cottage in the area. It was built during the war. The Summerville's were wonderful people with a beautiful daughter. Then, Mr. and Mrs. Jones, a jolly couple, left the place. Mr. Thornton died in a car accident. And then there was the retired colonel… I forget his name. His son joined the services, too. Those were the original residents of that neighborhood: the Founding Fathers! They were all fine people, and I served as a maid for many of those households. They gave you proper respect if you did your job well."

"That must have been many years back?" enquired Chelsie with some trepidation.

"Oh yes! Long, long ago and full of life in those days." The old lady replied with evident pride.

"Do you know any of the current residents?" Chelsie asked.

"No, missus! I daresay not," the woman replied haughtily. "And why should I? These days, people come and go. The cottages have turned into kind of inns, you see. And no one cares for anyone nowadays."

"I understand your daughter served in some of these cottages as a maid?"

"Yes, Emily has got my strain. She is dutiful, firm, and committed. Everyone is satisfied with her work, not only here but in New Orleans, too. Mr. Jenson said it was a good thing…"

Chelsie interrupted her. "Emily worked in a cottage by the lake, where the forest begins. Do you know anything about that cottage?" she asked.

"The one by the lake…why, that was a beautiful cottage, but now it lies vacant. It wasn't very old, however. It wasn't there when I was working. It was built much later by an Irishman from Washington. He returned to Washington, they say."

"Did Emily serve the Irishman?"

"The Irishman? Heaven's no! That was a miserable family to serve. Emily was there later when that young man lived there. Ah, the poor thing! He was a gentleman, firm, a man of character. He's not very old… he'd have been your age. Most unfortunate tragedy, so it was!" The old lady shook her head in pity.

"What?" Chelsie anticipated she was near the moment of reckoning.

"The man was engaged to a bubbly young lady, they say. I never had a chance to meet her, however. They had long been in a relationship and were to marry that summer. But the wedding never happened. It was unfortunate indeed… no one knows why, but she took a mouthful of pills the night before the wedding. She didn't wake up again. Lord knows what had passed between them. And no, that's not the end of the tragedy. The strong fellow broke down like a bunch of reeds…and dived into the lake that night. Can you imagine? The next day was their wedding, but here he was, all alone, his fiancé dead, and what does he do but end his life." She shook her head. "It was a real tragedy."

"How long ago did this happen?" asked Chelsie.

"Oh, I could still walk around then and used to visit the church. About five years, I think."

"No one else has stayed in the cottage since?"

"No, it's vacant, and Emily stopped working as a maid after that. Of course, now that she's in New Orleans…"

"Can you tell me something more about this man?" Chelsie interjected. "What was his name?"

"No missus, I don't remember the name at all. I knew the old people well, but not the new ones. Now, this guy, I did know the name…but cannot recall it now. His parents used to stay near his cottage, I heard. I don't know if they are still there. My memory isn't what it used to be, you see! But you can visit here when Emily comes next, and she'll surely tell you."

"One last thing, did Emily ever say if he played the harmonica?"

"Ah, I don't know, missus! But I can ask my daughter the next time she gets in touch."

Chelsie thanked Louisa and left. As she trudged back home, she didn't know what to make of the information. It hadn't made things particularly clear.

****

As she passed by the woods, she looked inside with some expectation. She almost hoped David might be there, waiting for Chelsie to accompany him for a walk inside the secluded forest. Of course, it wasn't dark today. It was barely early afternoon. Wearing the checkered men's shirt, Chelsie felt more confident today.

Walking along the shores of the lake, she shuddered to think that the man who lived in their cottage had ended his life in the tranquil waters. Instead of heading straight towards their cottage after passing the lake, Chelsie visited Bill. It hadn't occurred to her earlier that Bill might know about the past occupants of their cottage. It would also be a pleasant surprise for Bill Chelsie to visit him.

She turned left towards Bill's place. It was some distance away, and the stretch was secluded, shadowed by the woods along the road. A little ahead, she saw an abandoned old car. It was dusty, and creepers had started to entwine it all around. The driver's side door was open. As Chelsie approached the car, low but clear notes of the lilting harmonica could be heard. The sound was coming from inside the car.

The tune gave her goosebumps, but Chelsie was more courageous today than usual. It might have been the shirt or because she wanted to believe David was just around the corner to rescue her. In any case, she peered inside the open car door. An old tape recorder lay in the dilapidated front seat. She walked around to the front of the car and froze. On the windshield, painted in white, the following words stared at her: C. C., UNFRIEND ME NOT.

CHAPTER 13

Though the car incident shook her, Chelsie gathered herself together and rang the doorbell at Bill's house. After she saw the graffiti on the windshield, her initial impulse was to scout the place and locate the person responsible. But her courage dwindled, and she had walked away as fast as she could from the scene.

Standing on Bill's doorstep, she wondered if she should tell him about the harmonica affair and ask for his opinion. She wasn't too keen on the idea – primarily because she wasn't sure if David was behind the whole thing. Her plot had spilled over to real life, and keeping the fiction apart from reality was getting more complex. It would require a lot of explanation to make someone else understand the situation. Although she wasn't too eager to discuss the entire story, she shared parts with Bill.

Bill flashed a massive smile of surprise as he opened the door. But in a moment, his smile gave way to wide-eyed disbelief. He stared at Chelsie with an inexplicable look, and, for a moment, both stood speechless at the door, his baffling gaze and her not knowing how to respond. Chelsie contemplated whether she had done the right thing by visiting him. She'd always been curious about the attention and care Bill showered her with. In happier times, it was the subject of harmless jokes between Brian and herself. Now, encountering this surprising reaction from Bill, she hesitated before stepping in. She surmised he wasn't staring at her face but rather at her body – her breasts.

Chelsie finally broke the uncomfortable stalemate with an affected, "Hi!"

Bill responded with a hasty smile, lifted his eyes to meet hers, and stepped aside.

"Come in, lady. What a great surprise," he said.

Chelsie entered and looked around. It was a tidy place. Although Bill lived alone, he seemed to be a neat and organized man. Everything was where it should be, and the house appeared to have everything needed to lead a contented retired life in the country. She settled on the couch as Bill perched on the edge of a vintage wooden chair.

Distracted by the unusual welcome, Chelsie was at a loss for words. She contemplated how to broach the topic she'd come to discuss. But Bill's stare wasn't typical, and Chelsie decided she shouldn't give the impression she had come to ask for his help. Instead, she tried to sound as if it were a casual visit.

"You're a tidy person," she said chattily.

Bill smiled. Regaining his poise to some extent, he said, "I was expecting both of you. Why alone?"

Did this query hint at something? Chelsie wondered. Was he happy to find her alone? Was he aware of the recent rift in their marital life? Had Brian confided in him? She knew Brian held Bill in high esteem.

"I needed some fresh air and went for a walk. We've wanted to visit you for a while, but my writing has reached a crucial stage, and I am avoiding distractions." Chelsie sounded apologetic.

"Contrary to popular belief, writing is a demanding job." Bill nodded. "You're helplessly lost within the intrigues of your plot and faced with innumerable dilemmas no one else can sort out for you."

The words rang so prophetic that Chelsie was overwhelmed. She let down her guard and became more relaxed.

"So true," she said with a sigh. "I've been stuck at one point or another."

"Writer's block?" Bill smiled. "I'm sure the country air will do you a lot of good. You seldom go out."

"Back in the city, I was always the outgoing type. I loved to go out and meet people. Most of my day was spent interacting, meaning I wrote only late at night. Socializing gave me the necessary inspiration, which I put on paper at night. Brian, on the other hand, was reserved and introspective. He'd rather stay home with his favorite book than attend a talk delivered by the author. But out here in the country, things have changed. He's the one who has already traversed the entire region – like those vintage explorers – plotting and mapping the area. He knows most people around here; he knows the forest well – all this while I'm cooped up at home wrestling with my characters every day!"

Chelsie stopped for breath. She was surprised she'd expressed so much to Bill, but it felt good. Almost as good as it had felt the night she shouted at Brian during dinner.

Bill looked at her with sympathy. "I understand. But Brian has a unique side to his character that feels more at ease among nature. He is more rustic inside than people think he is. How he has adapted to the countryside, his dedication to teaching, and his attachment to the trees and birds in the woods go so well with his personality. You're the best judge, but I think he has found more focus in his life here than in the city."

Chelsie realized she hadn't thought about Brian for a long time. It was surprising how incisive Brian's observation was. She remembered how her agent suggested they move to the country, and Brian was more enthusiastic about the plan. She remembered how he scouted for the suitable cottage in the right surroundings with zeal. At the time, Chelsie thought Brian was going through all the trouble for her sake. Now, she felt he'd done it for his own. She didn't know whether she should be happy or sad about it. Her feelings for Brian had reached a plateau where it was easier to go downhill than reach new heights. David was her hero – not Brian. Had Brian ever been her hero? She was troubled that she didn't have an answer.

She tossed her head impatiently, shaking off the disturbing thought. Changing the topic, she said, "I'd like to see your garden."

"Certainly!" Bill rose from the chair. "But do come in the morning someday. The garden seems far more beautiful in the early hours. There are birds, butterflies... and the sunlight assumes a different color then."

They walked towards the garden, Bill leading and Chelsie following. As they stepped out into the open, Bill turned around.

"Is that Brian's shirt you're wearing?" he asked.

Chelsie stopped in her tracks, so surprised her mouth gaped. This would require a lot of explaining, and even then, she might come across as a crazy freak. She gulped. The most accessible reply was to pretend it was Brian's. So she forced a smile, although she wasn't sure how effective it was, and nodded. Then, sensing a nod might not seem convincing enough after the surprised look on her face, she added: "Umm, yes. I wear them often."

Bill didn't respond; he just turned and walked into the garden ahead of her. As she followed, Chelsie realized her mistake. Any sensible person would notice the size difference between herself and her husband. Bill, being a draftsman in his professional life, was sure to possess a discerning eye where shapes and measurements were concerned. She knew Bill had seen through her. She felt like running away, yet she was curious why Bill had asked in the first place.

She couldn't concentrate as Bill showed her different varieties of flowering plants in his garden. For one thing, Chelsie wasn't much of a botanist, and given her present state of mind, the task was more difficult. The fruit-bearing plants in his small orchard were easier to identify. The garden was lovely, and Chelsie would have sincerely liked to spend some time there, enjoying the neatly manicured lawn and looking at the dazzling array of colorful blossoms. But all she thought of was the embarrassing situation she had put herself in.

She realized the reason she had visited Bill in the first place and the abrupt query he'd made were directly related. They were different facades of the same problem. Knowing who had lived in their house before them would sort out the mystery of the trunk in the attic. Although she realized with some embarrassment, it wouldn't explain her peculiar fondness for the clothes.

Bill continued the tour of his garden like a trained guide, explaining each plant's name and unique features. He was thorough, yet his voice belied a lack of involvement.

It became evident that the only way out of this delicate mess was to confide everything in Bill. He was genuine, and whatever idiosyncrasies he had in his attitude towards Chelsie didn't seem harmful or malicious. Bill was the only person in this place where she'd established mutual trust and friendship.

They turned towards the house after covering the entire garden. By now, the sun had slanted towards the far side of the lake. The lake wasn't visible from Bill's house, however.

As soon as they stepped indoors, Chelsie said, "I'm sorry, Bill; I lied about the shirt. It doesn't belong to Brian… you can see it's too big for him. I found it in a trunk stowed away in our attic."

CHAPTER 14

Bill stood transfixed on the spot. His gaze roamed over Chelsie's body – very slowly, very tenderly. She felt like he was caressing her with his eyes. Then, they finally rested on hers. Coming from outdoors, there wasn't much light inside. Bill's antique furnishings and the dying daylight fashioned a lazy chiaroscuro on the wooden flooring. It would have seemed that time stood still if not for the constant ticking of the grandfather clock.

It was Chelsie who spoke first.

"I wanted to know certain things and thought you were the best person to ask."

Bill remained silent.

"Did you know the people who stayed in our cottage before we moved in?" she asked.

Bill nodded.

"Wonderful," Chelsie felt satisfied for the first time that afternoon. "So you know! We should have asked you sooner. Who were they?"

With a gesture of his hand, Bill motioned her to follow him. He walked across the hall towards the room's door opposite the entrance. Chelsie followed hesitantly and then stopped at the doorway to his bedroom. Bill entered the room and approached the chest of drawers on the left wall. Chelsie stood outside. She heard the click of a switch, and the lights came on. A moment later, Bill returned to the doorway with something in his hand. Before Chelsie could focus on the object, she noticed tears rolling down Bill's cheeks.

"What's the matter?" she asked with genuine concern.

Bill held out the item. It was a framed photograph of a handsome young man about thirty-five. He stared at the camera with bright eyes and with a perfect head of hair fringing his broad forehead. The man had charm and personality written all over him.

"This is my son," said Bill in a choked voice. "He lived in your cottage."

Sequences and consequences whirled in Chelsie's mind as she stood a mute spectator. She understood the reason for Bill's tears because now she knew the identity of the man Mrs. Fenton said had jumped in the lake.

Bill walked to the living room and placed the photo on the low coffee table between the couches. Then he dropped down on the nearest couch as if drained of all energy. Chelsie followed him, settling on the opposite couch, and waited for him to recover. The lamps were off in the living room, and the hall remained dark, but the light from the bedroom glided through the open doorway and formed an illuminated rectangle that reached the foot of the coffee table where the framed picture sat.

Bill cleared his throat and repeated, "Yes. My son lived in your cottage. He's dead."

"I'm sorry," Chelsie said in a low voice. "I never meant to…"

"It's all right," Bill said. "That was five years ago. The cottage has been unoccupied ever since. I'm unsure why you want to know its history, but I have no problem speaking about my son. He was a promising young fellow. He trained as an architect and established his firm in the city. I'm a draftsman myself, and I can tell with certainty that he had a creative streak and quickly made his mark in the profession. He executed projects for important clients but was extremely independent and had several other interests. He was interested in art history, studied classical languages like Latin, learned French, and played the violin. But his nature was multifaceted. On the one hand, he was inclined to fine arts; on the other, he was interested in adventure. He watched action movies avidly, learned horse riding, and even wanted to become trained in Japanese martial arts. That never happened, though."

Chelsie felt a tingle down her spine as she listened to the qualities Bill's son possessed.

"Another of his quirks was his passion for country living. Although he had his consultancy in the city, he preferred staying here and buying the lake cottage. He received full support from his girlfriend. She was a wonderful person. Born and raised in the country, she studied architecture with my son. She was extremely enthusiastic and so full of life. They were a perfect couple! They planned to participate in adventure sports in South Africa after their marriage. They would have gone earlier, but my son had this strange fear of water…swimming was one activity he had never learned. But

Julia said – that was her name, by the way – Julia said she would teach him how to swim, and then they'd go. It never happened."

Bill paused.

"So they didn't get married?" Chelsie asked softly after a few moments. She knew they hadn't, but it was the only thing she could say now.

"No, but they lived together. Julia loved the cottage and wanted to start something for the town children on her own once they got married. Everything had been arranged, and the wedding was set, but I soon realized things weren't going well, and they were having problems. I guessed it was something personal but didn't know what exactly. Perhaps it would have been easier had my wife been alive. Julia went to her parents during Easter, and I thought a breakup was imminent. But she returned after a week, and things appeared to have been sorted out. The wedding day was near, and I expected all troubles to dissolve post-marriage. But the evening before, Julia took an overdose of sleeping pills." Bill paused momentarily and said, "It was late evening, and we rushed her to the hospital. But as we drove, it became obvious she wouldn't wake up. The cops wanted to question my son, but he was inconsolable… so they decided to wait. While Julia did the unthinkable, my son was here with me, sitting right where you're sitting. The sheriff knew me and my family well and said the questioning could wait until the next morning. They made basic inquiries, and I brought him home with me, leaving their cottage under lock and key. On our way home, he muttered, 'It was my fault,' a few times. He grew silent after that and fell asleep, or so I thought. I had decided to keep a vigil but dozed off in the wee hours. When I woke, it was almost seven o'clock. He was nowhere to be seen. I found the keys to his cottage missing and rushed over there. The cottage was unlocked, meaning he had returned either at night or early in the morning. He was an early riser anyway.

We couldn't find him anywhere in the cottage or around the place. Not until later, that is. They found his body floating in the lake around ten in the morning."

By the time Bill finished telling his story, darkness had engulfed the world outside. Inside, the oblong light languidly spreading on the floor glowed constantly and as indifferent as ever. The clock ticked. Bill sat with his head lowered, breathing heavily.

All Chelsie could utter was, "I'm sorry."

Bill raised his head slowly. "It's all right," he said.

"We'll never know what went wrong," Chelsie whispered, primarily to herself.

"No, we won't, and that's disturbing because they were made for each other. Why did you want to know who lived in the cottage?" Bill's voice sounded like he had finally grasped his emotions.

"Because strange things are happening," murmured Chelsie.

"Like?" Bill raised his eyebrows.

"Like someone playing a harmonica around our cottage in the dead of night. Brian and I even saw the guy from a distance one moonlit night. He was standing on the wooden jetty by the lake."

Genuinely shocked into silence, Bill finally said, "So that's why you and your husband asked me whether anyone played the harmonica!"

"Yes."

"Did this happen often?"

"Not really… just twice around the house at night, and once, while we were returning from the fair, it played from within the woods. That was in the evening. And today, while coming to your place, I saw a deserted old car by the roadside – just next to the chestnut trees near the clearing…"

"A green car?" Bill interrupted.

"Yes," she nodded.

"It belonged to Mr. Wilson. Their cottage is beyond the chestnuts. They moved away last summer. But tell me about the car."

"Someone left an old-fashioned tape recorder in it… one that plays audio cassettes. It was playing the same harmonica tune. I didn't see anyone around."

Bill sprang up as fast as an old man could. "Let's go and check it out. I'll take a flashlight. You can stay here if you want to."

He turned on the lights in the living room. The hall seemed to expand as the oblong of luminosity vanished from the floor.

"In all probabilities, you won't find anyone now," Chelsie said. "Oh, and someone scribbled 'unfriend me not' in white paint on the windshield."

"Strange. We'll check it out. By the way, have you thought of calling the police?"

"Brian wanted to, but I was against it."

"Why? It would be prudent to get the cops involved."

"I thought it would sound silly…" Chelsie hesitated. "Besides, the person was doing no harm and…" she stopped short of saying she thought it might have been David serenading her.

"If you want, I'll talk to my friend, the sheriff." Bill offered. "This sounds like stalking."

"So kind of you! Yes, Brian suspected someone might be stalking me…"

Suddenly, her cell phone rang.

It was Brian.

"Where are you, honey?" he enquired anxiously.

Chelsie always stayed out alone after sundown since they had moved. It wasn't that she felt incredibly unsafe, but there had been no reason to. Today, she'd planned to return before Brian came home from work.

"I'm visiting Bill," she said on the phone. "I'll be back in fifteen minutes."

"Oh, okay. I went for a walk, and then it got dark…"

"Don't worry. He'll accompany me home with his flashlight." She laughed.

Relieved, Brian hung up.

"Of course, I will," said Bill. "I also want to check the car. I wouldn't say I like the way things are shaping up. We must nab this harmonica freak."

"There's something else," Chelsie said in an uncertain voice. "There's a trunk in our attic filled with men's clothes. Apparently, they belonged to your son."

Bill looked at her in askance. She hesitated and spoke again.

"I feel a strange compulsion to wear them. I'm drawn to them, and I can't explain it." She paused but forced herself to continue. "It's almost a sensuous pleasure wearing them…"

Her voice trailed off. Bill looked at her shirt with a tender, caring gaze. Now she knew he wasn't staring at her bosom.

Bill turned and entered the bedroom, returning with something in his hands.

"Since the first day I saw you, my wonder never ceased," he said. "And this is why."

He stretched his hand out. It was another framed photo, but this time of a young woman wearing a man's checkered shirt. Chelsie was taken aback to see how much she resembled her!

"This is Julia," Bill said before she could ask anything. "Don't ask me how two unrelated people can look identical and wear the same checkered shirt. It must be a freak of nature. I don't know whether it addresses the mystery concerning your fondness for my son's clothing. I truly have no answer."

Chelsie took the photograph and looked intently. Despite the best of efforts, her hands trembled.

"Come on, it's getting late," Bill said.

Chelsie got up and moved towards the coffee table, photograph in hand. She put it down next to the photo of Bill's son.

"I wish I could have met them – Julia and your son... what's his name, by the way?"

"David," said Bill.

CHAPTER 15

Bill walked her home with his flashlight. On the way, they passed the abandoned green car. Its front door was no longer hanging open. Bill pointed the flashlight inside and peered. As expected, no tape recorder was inside except for clear imprints on the dust-covered front seat, which implied recent activity. The writing, however, remained on the glass.

"C.C. is meant for you," said Bill. "This can't be ignored any longer. I'll talk to the sheriff first thing in the morning."

Chelsie didn't speak. She was in no condition to think, although physically, she felt better now. But her mind was burdened with too many thoughts and hence refused to work. This had been her most hectic day so far.

Bill bade her good night at the gate. Although Chelsie invited him to come in, he refused. He understood she was in a volatile state of mind and needed some time in private to gather herself.

"Tell Brian not to worry about the harmonica player," he said before he left. "My friend will take care of that. I'll come tomorrow or the day after with an update."

A very anxious Brian opened the door. He got even more concerned to find his wife worn out. He noticed the checkered shirt Chelsie was wearing but didn't comment on it. Brian prepared dinner and set the table as she changed, washed, and finally stretched her legs over the living room couch.

"Come and sit," she called out. "Dinner can wait. I've got something important to discuss."

Brian put the plates down on the table and sat on the couch.

"I went to town today," she said.

"To town? All by yourself? I thought you said you had visited Bill?"

"Yes, but that was later in the afternoon. I went to town a little before noon."

"You met the maid, I suppose? Emily?" Brian asked.

"No, I didn't…or rather, couldn't. She took a job somewhere in New Orleans and is gone. But her mother was there, and she had a great deal of information. She spoke a lot of rubbish but also mentioned a young man living here at this cottage until five years back. She couldn't tell me his name, though, or provide any details."

"You think this might be our man? The one who plays the harmonica?" asked Brian, warming up to the plot.

"No. This person died. He jumped into the lake because his fiancé committed suicide."

"He committed suicide as well? That's awful, but it doesn't solve our problem. By the way, did you walk to town by yourself?"

"Yes, all the way there and back. Enough exercise for one day. But listen. There's more to the story. I decided to ask Bill. I've finally found him."

Her eyes glistened unusually bright, her lips trembled, and her breath came short and fast. Unable to comprehend the sudden surge of passion, Brian asked, "Whom?"

"David!" Chelsie almost cried out loud with the joy of serendipitous discovery. "Now I know who he is. David is real, as I've always told you."

Brian waited to hear more before reacting.

"Bill's son lived here. He's David."

"What do you mean he's David? Bill has a son?"

"The guy who lived here... the one who jumped into the lake – he was Bill's son. He owned this cottage. His name was David, and you wouldn't believe how remarkably close he was to my concept of David."

Abruptly pausing now and then to catch her breath, nostrils flaring in excitement, Chelsie relayed all she'd learned about David and his ill-fated love story. Brian listened with interest, but when it was over, he leaned back into the couch and released one long breath.

Then he said, "Going by your account, David was real. He's not here anymore."

Chelsie wasn't too happy with his interpretation. The fact she had found David so close to her, the resemblance she bore to the love of his life, and the waves of other surprises that had incessantly battered her senses throughout the day no longer allowed her to care for logic or reason. David was there; she was his lady – that was all she knew.

Meanwhile, Brian had been running the facts through his mind. Finally, he said, "Well, all this information does help clear up a part of the mystery. Like, now we know why Bill always gave you that curious look or who the clothes in the attic belonged to. But this doesn't explain our two major questions—the first you raised. You think your novel is getting written by itself, and we have no explanations for that – although I still firmly believe it's all your imagination. The brain works in strange ways, and being overworked, you must be forgetting portions you've scripted."

Chelsie sat in vexed silence – her dislike for Brian meandered its way back into her heart. Brian must be jealous that David was working as her co-author on the novel. And it was clear to her that her husband couldn't stand David communicating with her. Of course, she hadn't mentioned anything about the mystery co-author to Bill. That was partly premeditated – she was unsure what he might think – and partially because the random twists and turns throughout the day had been too distracting for her. After a while, she dryly asked, "And what is the other major question?"

"Yes, that is my real concern. Who is the harmonica asshole that keeps following us?"

Chelsie had utterly forgotten to tell Brian about the abandoned car, the tape recorder, and the graffiti on its windshield. The delight upon the discovery of David had made the harmonica episode inconsequential to her for the moment. Until today, she had a faint hope it might be David serenading her. But she knew David didn't play the harmonica. Moreover, the message on the car's windshield didn't gel with the dynamics David and she shared through the manuscript. That would have been a more natural communication channel for him rather than scribbling on dilapidated cars with paint cans.

She informed Brian about the car and told him how Bill had promised to extend his help. Brian got more involved and displayed greater interest.

"Two things are clear from today's incident," he declared with conviction. "One, this guy has indeed been stalking you. Your initials make it obvious."

"Bill agrees," Chelsie said.

"Naturally, however, point number two is more crucial. 'Unfriend me not' suggests this is a person you have recently unfriended on Facebook, and it didn't sit well with him. He might be looking for an opportunity to strike back."

"I never felt this guy meant any harm," Chelsie protested.

"True. Yet it's obvious he won't let you live in peace. This harmonica thing might be his way of getting back at you – troubling you psychologically."

Chelsie knew it was possible.

"Have you unfriended anyone recently?" Brian asked.

"Possible, but I don't remember anyone in particular. Still, I'll check my Facebook history and let you know."

"Do that. We must let the sheriff know if we find anything suspicious there."

Chelsie nodded.

Brian was thankful Bill had offered help and, at the same time, was much relieved to find out Chelsie had finally ceded to the idea of getting the sheriff involved.

"I'll visit Bill myself first thing tomorrow morning. He's a genuine person and cares about us. I'm glad we've got such an exemplary neighbor. He's been through a lot and yet has composure and compassion."

Chelsie agreed with Brian but thought only a perfect father like Bill could have raised a genius like David!

Comforted with the positive turn of events, Brian enthusiastically stood up from the couch.

"Let's eat! You must be famished."

Chelsie watched as he rushed to complete the dinner. Somehow, she couldn't tolerate the complacency Brian exuded after learning the police were getting involved. He was too mundane. Too enclosed within his perimeter of order and logic, too short-sighted and dispassionate to be the perfect man for a woman as creative, passionate, and visionary as she was. She desperately wanted to deal with one fatal prick to his bubble.

She said in a measured tone, "Brian, I still think David is real."

Brian stopped what he was doing but didn't turn around. He resumed his task and, without turning to face her, he said, "Okay, honey, but think it over. If David were alive, his writing on your laptop would mean he'd broken into the house. However...." Brian paused.

"What?" Chelsie asked in a stern voice.

"However, David is dead. So, his writing suggests ..." This time, he deliberately left the sentence incomplete.

The table was ready, and, hearing no response from his wife, he turned to an empty room.

CHAPTER 16

Chelsie was quiet for the next couple of days. Each morning after breakfast, she dutifully sat at her desk in the study and remained there until lunch. Afterward, she would roam distractedly through the house – stopping here and there, observing each room and every item of furniture with curiosity, and probably appearing to an onlooker as though she was noticing things for the first time. But Brian didn't return until late afternoon, and no one was watching her. She went around the house thinking of how things were shaped when two passionate lovers lived there until five years back.

She hadn't written much because she was in a quandary regarding the plot of her novel. She was getting too involved with the narrative, and she knew it. As the creator, she needed to maintain a clinical detachment to make the work flawless. But she realized she could no longer remain aloof after realizing she lived in David's house. This was his dream cottage – as Bill had said. This was where he had spent passionate moments with Julia – whom Chelsie closely resembled. She'd felt so restless and charged up whenever she had been alone in the house, and it started after Brian took up his teaching job. Was she being influenced by the unseen presence of a strapping young man so full of life but alive no more? As Brian suspected, was she being stalked – not by the man outside but by one within? She wasn't afraid at the thought – not at all! Instead, she felt turned on by the idea; a kind of exhibitionistic pleasure urged her on whenever alone.

Although Brian had noticed the sudden change in her attitude, he didn't interfere. He was more involved in the pursuit of the suspected stalker. He'd contacted Bill the day after Chelsie returned from his house.

"You should have told me about this fellow earlier," Bill had complained mildly to Brian. "As a veteran resident, I must get things sorted out for new dwellers in the neighborhood."

"I know, Bill, but Chelsie wasn't too eager to share the story. She feels the man doesn't intend to do any harm."

"Whatever the case might be, it can't go on. As a successful author, your wife is a public figure, and you never know what these psychos are after. Nowadays, you have the internet, Facebook, Twitter, and social media, as they call it… and you can't stay away from it like a Salinger or a Harper Lee. It's become easier for strangers to track you down. Let's not take this lightly. I'll introduce you to my friend, Sheriff Trott."

The sheriff was an amicable elderly person – due to retire in a year. He listened attentively and asked if Brian wanted to lodge a formal complaint.

"Is it necessary at this stage? What do you suggest?"

"A formal complaint would get my force acting right now, but I don't think there's reason to panic. I suggest you keep my number and call me when you feel like it. However, file a formal complaint the moment any further incidents occur."

"I'm sure your men will remain alert," said Brian.

"They always are." Sheriff Trott grinned. "It all depends on how soon events are reported."

Brian was a much-relieved man afterward. The following Saturday, he proposed going out to eat.

"Let's go to The Smoking Embers," he said.

It was the one good local restaurant in town. They had eaten there once before, and Chelsie had liked the food. The menu didn't offer a wide variety, but the taste was authentic. Brian was more concerned with ambiance, and it suited his taste.

He wasn't sure Chelsie would accept the invitation. He readied himself for a refusal even as he proposed the outing. To his surprise, Chelsie contemplated for a few minutes and replied, "Fine, let's go this evening."

Brian spent the rest of the day in a lighter mood than he'd been in for quite some time. The possible resolution of the mystery surrounding the harmonica-playing stalker, the knowledge Bill's son was the previous occupant of their cottage, Chelsie's tranquil mood, and now her agreeing to go out for dinner – all pointed to a possible end to the discord spoiling their relationship. He hoped things would return to normal – and they lead a fulfilling life together again, as they had done for so many years. Maybe Chelsie would emerge from impossible reveries and concentrate on her groundbreaking work of fiction. He'd get the opportunity to bask in the late summer sun and soak in the glorious beauty of the countryside.

His day passed merrily until he saw Chelsie dressed for the evening. She was wearing one of the checkered men's shirts from the attic trunk!

It was different from the ones she'd worn before. It had more green in the checks. Brian realized it might be long before his wife abandoned her daydreaming.

"Must you wear that tonight?" he asked.

"Why? Do you have a problem?" Chelsie shot back in a calm yet firm voice.

"Honey, you own lots of wonderful dresses you look great in. Why must you wear old, dusty hand-me-downs from a stranger?" Brian was being deliberately gentle as he spoke.

"I think I look great in these. I don't have checkered ones…. I think I'll buy a few." Chelsie replied.

Encouraged by her non-hostile attitude towards the much-debated topic, Brian said, "Fine, let's go buy some. If you wish, we can go shopping now, and dinner can wait."

"No, let's go to dinner. And I want to wear this shirt. It's a superb fit," she said as she patted her full bosom.

Brian cast a sidelong glance at her ripping figure – a form he knew well but now seemed as distant as a childhood memory. Not intent on spoiling the evening, he didn't argue. As they stepped onto the walkway, Chelsie said, "These clothes may be old, but very clean," she said. "Not dusty at all. Also, they belong to David. He's no stranger."

The image of Chelsie's shapely bottom encased within a pair of men's briefs crossed Brian's mind. Was she wearing them today, as well?

****

The Smoking Embers was located on the edge of town. To reach the town square, one had to go past the restaurant. Behind the eatery, the pathway wound north and headed towards the woods. Following the twists and turns in that direction, you'd reach the shortcut Chelsie and Brian had taken to the county fair. Despite the area being desolate, The Smoking Embers had a loyal clientele. By the time they got there, it was busy. The place tried to juxtapose the traditional tavern environment with cool chic. The muted earth tones, the airy interior adorned with dark woods, and the long, sleek bar festooned with epicurean literature combined to create an inviting dining space neither had expected. Back then, they'd decided to go often, but somehow that plan hadn't materialized. The strange turn of events and their rapidly diminishing level of communication made it so neither was in the right frame of mind to think of dining out; not until today, that was.

They settled at a table by the large glass window that overlooked the road to the woods. Brian ordered two cocktails and poured over the menu with a distinctly contrived enthusiasm. He was desperate to make the evening happy and tried to animate Chelsie – like a gawky teenager on his first date.

"Look… they've got some intricate preparations. This one here says roasted bone marrow topped with marinated anchovies, or you could have crisp Kurobuta pork belly with curried squash purée or even herb-roasted branzino bathed in cauliflower purée! Umm… sounds exotic."

He looked up to check Chelsie's expression. She sat silent with an amused yet distant look in her eyes.

"What would you like to order, honey?" he asked, handing the menu over to her.

"Anything will do. You decide." She wasn't exactly aloof, but she didn't seem involved.

Brian stretched over the table and strained to read the items on the menu in front of her.

"Why don't we order some Alaskan halibut? They serve it with roasted tomato, coconut milk curry, and creamy lentil potatoes."

"Sounds great, honey; you order it," she said.

"Or would you care for salmon with creamy kale? Or the grilled flatbread with Spanish chorizo… oh yes, we had it the last time. It was good, but I'd like to experiment with unknown dishes, like the top sirloin with bone marrow butter!" He looked up at Chelsie with the air of an explorer who had reached the lost city of Atlantis.

"That should be good," she replied.

Brian hunched down on the menu once again.

"I'd also like to order a salad," he said. "Which one would you prefer – chopped pulled chicken or Caesar?"

Now, she had to make a decision. "The Caesar should be good," she said, only to keep up with Brian's effort in choosing the evening's fare. He called for the waiter.

As she unmindfully chomped on pieces of salad, Brian finally succeeded in ordering the main course, which they ate in complete silence.

She was thinking of her first date… with David. She had scripted the chapter with much care and affection, yet David had randomly altered the manuscript, rewriting the chapter to create a much bolder effect. That scene, too, involved a cozy restaurant. Consciously looking around the interior of The Smoking Embers, Chelsie was a little surprised to find that her mysterious co-author had described a similar interior for the restaurant in the novel. Chelsie shivered in uncontrollable delight at the thought of wearing David's shirt right now. The warm rasp of the fabric against her eager skin felt stimulating. It was as if David was teasing her with a titillating embrace.

She hadn't written for a few days, nor had her co-author. The revelations about David, the torrid and amorous days he must have spent with his fiancé, the luscious Julia and her uncanny resemblance to Chelsie, and the final tragedy enacted within the confines of their cottage – everything had created a haze in her mind. It needed to be cleared up. She also needed to make up her mind. Was it some ghostly presence writing her novel? Who would believe this? She knew Amy and Linda wouldn't. That was why Chelsie hadn't said anything about the real David to her friends yet.

But absent-mindedly dining with Brian as if she were with a stranger, Chelsie decided her next course of action. There was no denying David – Bill's dead son – was the perfect person for her. She wanted him as much as he had wanted her – or Julia, whatever! There was no reason for her to shy away now – be he alive or dead. She decided to submit to his whims and let him complete the novel as he thought best. She was now confident David could write a mind-blowing romance that would take America by storm. She wanted him by her side professionally, emotionally, and physically. But to keep the channel of communication open between them, she had to continue the novel. Chelsie decided to resume writing the following day.

Brian, too, thought of the novel as he ate. He knew how much regard Chelsie had for her work, and it was disconcerting to notice she'd stopped working on the novel she'd placed such a high premium on. This was to be her magnum opus, and she had lost her focus. It was becoming more and more evident that Chelsie wasn't behaving normally. Seeing his bright and talented wife becoming an obsessive wreck hurt him deeply. Wasn't the countryside supposed to reintroduce them to calm, relaxed, and uncomplicated living? He rued what it had done instead. Should they consider going back to the city?

Forcing the uncomfortable train of thought away, Brian asked Chelsie, "What's for dessert?"

Jolted out of her reverie, Chelsie replied, "Anything is fine."

"There are quite a few options," said Brian, turning over the dessert menu. "However, I'd suggest choosing between cranberry caramel and chocolate mousse with sweet vanilla ice cream."

"Let's go for the mousse," Chelsie said, aware Brian had a sweet tooth.

After the momentary distraction, they lapsed into silence once more. They nibbled the chocolate mousse without really caring for its taste or quality.

"They also have sponge cake orange segments with white chocolate," Brian said in a monologue after another spell of silence. "We can order it next time."

As Chelsie contemplated her willingness to go out for a possible future dinner with Brian, they heard the harmonica playing outside.

It was on the other side of the glass window beside their table. It was dark out, the forest providing a nocturnal backdrop. Inside, the lights shone bright, and Brian instantly realized that although they couldn't identify the person, he must clearly see them. Pressing his nose to the glass, Brian thought he could see the man standing outside.

"Wait for me," he uttered as he jumped from his seat. He rushed across the restaurant, lunged through the swing door, and disappeared from Chelsie's sight.

Taken aback by the sudden events, Chelsie tried her best to look through the glass. She couldn't see but heard the melody breaking off mid-tone moments after Brian ran outside. People seated at other tables stared at her, and she considered walking out but thought it more prudent to stay put. Brian returned after about ten minutes of anxiously waiting, panting, and sweating. He slumped in his chair and placed a brown leather wallet on the table.

Once outside, Brian saw the man standing on the pavement by the restaurant window and playing a harmonica. Tall and well-built, it was the same guy they'd seen on the wooden jetty. He was in his early twenties – wearing a black high-neck full-sleeved jersey and gray cargo pants. He ran when he saw Brian.

"Stop, stop!" Brian had yelled, but the man kept running.

He took the road leading to the forest. Brian chased with all his might, but the guy was faster. He disappeared amidst the darkness in the woods, and Brian gave up. While returning, Brian discovered the wallet lying on the road.

Brian opened the wallet under the pendulum lampshade above their table and took out a driver's license. The wallet belonged to Nick Carter.

****

Back home, Chelsie opened her Facebook page.

"The 'Unfriend me not' scribble was a needle in the haystack, but now we've got a real clue," Brian said.

"Call the sheriff," Chelsie said in a timid tone. She was yet to get over the shock.

"Of course, I will, but first, let's see if we can find anything about this rogue. He must have been on your Facebook account. Check all the people you've unfriended recently."

They went through her history and, sure enough, discovered the suspect. It helped that they knew his name. Nick Carter was a young man of twenty-four, and Chelsie remembered him now. He'd been a crazed fan since he was a teen. These things happened, and being a romance writer, Chelsie knew her readers mostly belonged to a volatile, extremely impressionable age group. Her talent and beauty were a heady mix, and a few weren't uncommon to develop an infatuation. Nick started sending personal and intimate messages begging to meet her as time progressed. She never replied to his messages except for one-word replies early on. Later, when they became more and more obstinate and lurid, she avoided answering him altogether. Finally, she had no option but to unfriend him. She had never thought of getting the cops involved, as the entire episode seemed to be harmless and reflected her popularity among readers. Also, calling the cops might have generated bad publicity and spoiled her image.

Brian and Chelsie looked at the photos Nick had uploaded to his account. He was decidedly handsome – with a sharp nose, clean-shaven pointed chin, and piercing eyes hooded with joined eyebrows. A head of curly, unruly hair extended over his shoulders. From the hair and the broad-shouldered frame, they quickly identified him as the man on the jetty. In most pictures, he was surrounded by books or musical instruments; in two, he was seen posing with a harmonica.

As they saw the photos, both distinctly remembered seeing him at different promotional events she'd attended. He'd always been quite close to them – staring wide-eyed at every move she made and hanging on every word she said but never over-imposing. Not once had he spoken or approached her with any requests. Had he stalked her for years? Chelsie shuddered.

"What surprises me most is how he found out you were here," remarked Brian. "We never publicly announced your move, and Kevin is keeping the entire plan under wraps until the promotion for your new novel starts."

Chelsie nodded in silence.

"Either Nick is well-connected or extremely desperate," continued Brian. "We need to remain alert. I'll call the sheriff, and we'll meet him tomorrow morning to lodge a formal complaint and hand over the wallet."

Brian sighed as they switched off the lights and exclaimed, "At least one mystery is solved!"

Chelsie didn't say anything.

CHAPTER 17

Chelsie sat at her desk but didn't look at the laptop. She was thinking of dinner and the following events. She'd enjoyed it if she was dreaming about her date with David, but Brian talked way too much, and then along came Nick Carter to spoil the evening!

The entire harmonica affair had turned out to be a huge letdown. There are no romantic surprises, no supernatural mystery in it. It was neither David nor his forlorn spirit searching for his estranged lover. All in all, it left a sour aftertaste.

However, she still had her novel to complete. And she had full confidence in her co-author; David would never let her down. This novel had cost her in many ways. She had to leave the urban bustle she loved; circumstances had led her marriage to be in tatters, and she knew the pangs of being so near yet so far from her ideal – the type of man she had idolized since her teenage awakening of sexuality. All this is because of the novel. Chelsie turned her manuscript into a channel to vent her frustration and a creative, emotional, and erotic conduit.

She wrote in an agitated state, uncaring of the world around her. She didn't notice how summer was orchestrating one last grand finale outside before the curtains came down on the glorious season. As her story continued to unfold, she realized a sexual encounter with David was near, and her anticipation grew beyond imagination. Deviating from her original plans, she portrayed Chelsie, the character, with bolder strokes than initially conceived. She now wanted her to be outspoken and uninhibited – a heroine who would shock the mushy sentimentality of the regular romance reader. She had to convert her into someone capable of satisfying David and be satisfied in her own turn. She was almost metamorphosing into a female equivalent of David. She had Julia's traits – whatever Bill had said – and she was more than Julia. She was what the real David had wanted Julia to be. Chelsie imagined Julia not participating in the games of love the masculine David enjoyed, leading to discord between the couple. Was that the reason she killed herself? Was there a third person in the relationship? Whatever might have been, Chelsie didn't want her heroine to suffer on account of not expressing her desires adequately. She would even make her a slut if it suited her purpose.

Every day, her writing and language style got more lurid and explicit. She didn't consider her readers or her publisher. Like it or dump it, this tenth novel would be different from all romances ever written in America. The only concern was how her co-author was going to respond. A lot depended on it. Her co-author was now an integral part of the scheme of things, and there was no way the novel would be successful or complete without his cooperation. To her delight, David responded after a hiatus of a couple of days. The nocturnal additions to her manuscript resumed with a vigor that matched Chelsie's passionate urgency.

Soon, Chelsie began to draft sequences much removed from her original plot. They were unveiled invites for David to sensual gratification. Even while she typed them, Chelsie knew how they would spoil her story. But, to her surprise, he constantly reworked those portions and brought the narrative back on track. What started as a unidirectional joint venture had evolved into a game where Chelsie was perpetually deviating from the matrix to pour her heart out, and her mystery co-author kept the story going – all the while indirectly acknowledging her lustful messages. Her anxiety regarding using bold language was substantially alleviated when she found David responding with equal audacity. It never failed to amaze Chelsie how seamlessly David's language merged with hers.

Chelsie began to behave more normally – like someone who had just returned from a vacation, rejuvenated. Life was good.

She called Amy and Linda via Skype one afternoon. She gushed about how David was responding to her advances and how she was finally feeling emotionally fulfilled as a woman.

"Wow… you're so imaginative!" Amy exclaimed.

"You have surpassed your creativity this time," Linda said.

Chelsie explained that she wasn't talking about her novel but her own emotions. David and Chelsie were made for each other; that mattered to her now.

"Go get it, girl!" Amy giggled. "Tell your man to give it to you, then write all about it. Your fans would go gaga. Only, I'm not sure what Brian will say."

"One of these days, I'm going to get David," responded Chelsie in a dreamy voice. "It'll be the best sex ever."

"Just can't wait to read about it." Amy was eager. "When do you plan to finish?"

"This isn't fiction; it's my life!"

"Stop trying to rattle me with literary dialogues. Tell me when you'll finish."

"I hope it's never finished."

"What bullshit is that?"

"I hope David and I go on writing together forever…"

Her words got drowned in peals of laughter and a series of catcalls from Amy.

Linda, too, joked about her obsession with David. However, she felt Chelsie wasn't conversing but baring her soul through one continuous monologue. After meaningless banter over David, Linda asked, "When do you plan to return?"

"Let me check with David," Chelsie replied.

"With Brian, you mean?" corrected Linda.

"Brian… why, no… I meant David!"

"Chelsie, I'm asking you in earnest."

"So?" Chelsie seemed surprised. "I'll have to plan the progress of my novel with David. He's writing with me, you know."

"For once, Chelsie, get out of your creative mode and try to descend to the level of lesser mortals like us." Linda became somewhat impatient.

"You don't get it," replied Chelsie. "I know making you understand will be difficult, but my life has changed. I'm unsure if I'll ever be my old self again."

Linda didn't feel comfortable with her answer but refrained from further arguments.

Her agent called the next day.

"How's our new romance getting along?" Kevin asked.

"With David, you mean?" Chelsie blushed.

"Yes, the rural romance between David and Chelsie. It's a great idea to make your heroine a cameo."

"David's great. He's helping me with the story."

"But of course," said Kevin. "Where would authors be if their characters didn't help them with the story?"

"I mean, David is my co-author and my protagonist."

"What is this, I hear? Some major alterations to the plot?" enquired Kevin in a more professional tone.

"Well, yes and no. The storyline has remained more or less the same since I last shared it with you. David prunes all redundant episodes whenever I try to stray from it and gets me back on track."

Kevin grunted an uncertain "Um-hum!" from the other end.

"You know, I'm in love with David, which will immensely help the narrative. I can now make it as explosive as possible. Wasn't that what you wanted? More sex, different kinds of sex? You'll have both in this book. David and I are going to turn the heat up, but beware! It might be too much for publisher Will Black to handle."

"But what are you saying about a co-author? You know the franchise won't allow any mention of co-creators."

"Oh no, although David is writing this with me, he won't claim anything. He lived here in our cottage. But he's dead now."

"He's what?" asked Kevin.

"He's dead. He died about five years back. But his input is invaluable. The way he synchronizes his style to mine…"

Kevin cut her short. "Chelsie, when do you plan to submit the first draft?" he asked sternly.

"I'm not sure," she replied extremely casually. "It all depends on how the plot turns out because David must make the final decision. There'll be this one climactic encounter between him and me… There will be a lot of sex in it. And then he'll have to draft his portion as well. That usually happens at night. So…"

"Just what are your plans?" Kevin interrupted again. "When do you think you'll return with a complete manuscript?"

Chelsie giggled like a schoolgirl. "What are you getting worked up for? You wanted a great romance. I promise I'll deliver you the greatest. I'm ready; it's all up to David now."

****

Was Chelsie a nymphomaniac? Brian pondered long as he watched daylight fade over the lake's waters. True, she was oversexed. It was also sure she'd had a couple of casual flings while in college. But since their marriage, he had always felt Chelsie was completely gratified after their sexual encounters. They were frequent, and she let loose her unbridled stallions of fantasy on every occasion. But Brian had always been an able rider and efficiently managed those stallions. He'd never felt inadequate, and, by the intimacy Chelsie shared, she wasn't dissatisfied with his performance.

Above everything, both of them valued the level of confidence they shared. It was emotional as well as physical. Each loved the abilities the other possessed, and they did not accuse each other of being nosey, distrustful, or disrespectful. Brian failed to understand how the plot of a novel could have turned Chelsie into a completely different person. Who is she after when she says David is the perfect man for her? How can she even think someone who died five years ago is writing her novel? Brian had to admit it was a strange coincidence that David had lived in their cottage, and that was the name Chelsie had chosen for her protagonist. It was also a quirk of fate that David's dead fiancé closely resembled Chelsie. But they were coincidences. Or was there something spooky in the house? Was Chelsie under the spell of some evil spirit? Brian would have never believed such a thing – he was rational and free of superstitions.

At the same time, it was true that his wife had changed. Brian longed for the lost days of intimacy and wanted to restore their relationship. It was evident from what she wrote in her manuscript and how she gushed over David that a deep sexual yearning lay unfulfilled within her. Was it affecting her psychological balance and her sanity?

By then, dusk had engulfed the lake. The cacophony of birds could still be heard from the treetops, but they would soon quiet down. After that, darkness and silence would rule the forest. Brian got up.

Just then, his cell phone rang, shattering the stillness of the evening.

It was Kevin Firth.

The elderly agent came to the point directly.

"Brian, can you tell me who David is?"

"He's a character in Chelsie's new novel," replied Brian.

"That much I know. But I called her this afternoon, and she said something about a co-author. This David is writing the novel alongside her…"

"So she seems to believe," said Brian.

"Ah, but what is really happening? There is a clause concerning Chelsie Crammer Romances, and the franchise won't tolerate a co-author." Kevin was getting worked up.

"I think the situation here is pretty volatile. I don't have much involvement in it."

"So it seemed to me. But is someone else actually working on the novel? I think I'll come down myself to discuss this with Chelsie. Yes, there's something else. Chelsie told me this David… or whoever is writing the novel with her… this person has been dead for years."

Brian didn't speak for a few moments. Then he said wearily, "It's a long story, Kevin. But I realize you need to know more than anyone else because it concerns the novel and the author you represent. Things have been under control for so long, but now I think it's taking a turn for the worse."

"What are you saying? Are you two okay?" Kevin's voice broke in consternation.

"I'll tell you everything," Brian said, lowering himself to the grass. Sitting by the lakeside and engulfed in the all-pervading darkness, he narrated the inexplicable gloom that had descended over their lives.

Kevin listened in absolute silence. After speaking, Brian said, "Listen, you need to act immediately. Take Chelsie to a psychiatrist. I can recommend one I know. You'll only need to drive a couple of hours to the city. Do this immediately and let me know what the doctor says."

Brian, too, had been thinking similarly and agreed wholeheartedly with what Kevin said.

Before hanging up, Kevin said, "Look, Brian, I've known Chelsie for as many years as you two have been married. Irrespective of our professional relationship, I always cared for you both in a way I can hardly explain. Do take care of her in the best possible way. I may be visiting your place early next week. Bye until then."

Within two days, Kevin Firth fixed an appointment with a leading psychiatrist. Brian knew he had to broach the topic tactfully, and that evening, he mentioned to Chelsie that he'd been feeling unusually stressed out.

"That stalker wrecked my nerves," said Brian. "I have lost mental peace ever since. I'm sure it's the same with you. Perhaps it would help immensely if we visited a psychiatrist. Kevin said he knew someone."

Chelsie thought it was a good idea and agreed. As Brian heaved a sigh of relief at her easy acquiescence, she suddenly asked, "Did Kevin call you?"

"Yes," he mumbled somewhat awkwardly.

Chelsie didn't ask any more questions. Deep down, she realized this was a plan to get her to see a psychiatrist. Surprisingly, she didn't oppose it.

"Finally, I can talk to a shrink and prove I'm not crazy and that David is real." Chelsie proclaimed.

Not wanting to start another fight, Brian remained silent.

****

Dr. Stuart Parker was a well-built man of around fifty, with a head full of golden hair and a charming smile. He wore thick-framed glasses that accentuated his bright and ever-smiling eyes. But as he listened to Brian, they lost their sparkle and became transfixed.

Chelsie and Brian had come to the doctor's office together, but Dr. Parker insisted he would like to talk with them individually first. Kevin had provided him with basic information, and he spoke with Brian first. When Brian finished his side of the story, the doctor nodded briefly.

"On the face, this sounds like a classic case of dissociative identity disorder," he finally spoke. "The person is behaving like two distinct personalities and distancing oneself while acting like the other."

"How serious is that?" Brian enquired with concern.

"We project different personae to different people. You say she deliberately wears men's clothing?"

"Yes, she wears them fully, knowing they belonged to a guy. But it's not just any clothing… only items in the attic."

"Can you say with some certainty that your wife never saw the name David inscribed on the trunk of clothes or any other article in your house?" Dr. Parker asked.

"I haven't seen it anywhere, and she never mentioned how she hit upon the name, but I'm not sure."

"The name might have unconsciously stuck in her mind, to be used for her hero later," conjectured the doctor. "In this case, the similarity between the real and the fictional David is the only unclear part to me. It could be coincidental, however. Otherwise, her condition displays common symptoms."

"There's no cause for concern then?"

"Certainly not. It has existed for ages, and everyone has had some amount. Previously, we called it multiple personality disorder or, more commonly, split personality. The gravity of the condition depends on the underlying cause and the extent to which it occupies the patient's mind. I'll talk to your wife before drawing early conclusions."

Chelsie went in after Brian left the room. She didn't have much to say, and the doctor didn't ask her anything related to her condition. He chatted about her books and the novel currently in progress. He also mentioned the Nick Carter incident to understand Chelsie's perception of the event better. She spoke with ease. Towards the end of the interview, she casually asked, "Doctor, do you think I am writing as David?"

The handsome doctor focused his twinkling eyes on hers, remained quiet for a few seconds, and gave his winsome smile.

"Probably, yes," he said. "The other possibilities are too fantastic. It could be the work of some paranormal presence, but would you willingly buy that idea? Or else it might have been an obsessed fan who is also a brilliant writer and matches your style to perfection – but does that sound plausible? More importantly, do you think it would be easy for an outsider to access your laptop regularly?"

The doctor called Brian in.

"Look, these things happen. Perfectly normal men and women may behave differently at different times under various stressful situations. First, we need to eliminate all possibilities of stress from your life. Stop overworking, eat, sleep, and enjoy your country stay. I'm sure a successful writer like you will come up with another brilliant novel. I'll prescribe medicine that will help. Take them for a few months, and you'll notice a difference."

CHAPTER 18

W as it day or night? Chelsie couldn't distinguish with certainty, and she didn't care. All the curtains were drawn, and the diffused light seeping in could signify dawn or dusk. How long she was lying in bed? Was she hungry? It wasn't obvious. Was she sleepy? She didn't know.

She hovered in an indefinite state of suspended consciousness. Mornings have been that way since she started the medicines. They were effective; her anxiety had lessened. Her days had become more relaxed, and the nights were spent in sound slumber. Only getting up in the mornings was a little tricky as it took some time for her senses to reoccupy her system after a nocturnal sabbatical. During that period, she resigned to a state of inactivity and waited for her body to gather momentum, just the thing she was doing. The last couple of days, she slept right through the morning. Not wanting to disturb her, Brian ate breakfast alone, and only when it was time for him to leave for work would he wake her up and serve breakfast and coffee in bed. Not that she overcame the stupor even after that. On some days – like today – after Brian left, she'd take another short nap until midday. It helped to refresh her. She'd get up and sit lazily by the window at her study for half an hour and then take her lunch. Afterward, she'd open her laptop and work until tall shadows crept through the window.

She and Brian would watch TV or browse books and magazines in the evening. Conversation lost its edge between them quite some time back. She'd hit the bed soon after dinner as the medication started working. Initially, she found the persistent drowsiness disturbing. Except for the stupor, she was perfectly fit, which made her dazed state even more unsettling. Dr. Parker had assured her that her system would get accustomed within a fortnight, and her sluggishness would gradually disperse. It had only been seven days. Nevertheless, it was apparent that the drug-induced languor had soothed her frayed nerves. Dr. Parker was right. She needed the break. The novel was getting too demanding.

The novel! A deluge of thought came rushing to her. Was Dr. Parker correct? Was her co-author a figment of her imagination? It was impossible. She might have turned somewhat neurotic, but she was still an author – a very able one! She might have become temporarily exhausted and emotionally drained, yet she was alert. She knew it. She knew well enough by the expertise gathered through years of laborious writing that she wasn't typing the nightly rejoinders to her manuscript. Although it was true that whoever added the portions had an uncanny style like hers, it was someone else and not her.

The conclusive proof was how the narrative progressed between the authors as if through a sequence of ripostes. She'd bring the plot to the precipice of some impending crisis and leave it there

— waiting for her co-author to resolve it — and sure enough, her anonymous collaborator would always solve predicaments with the best possible solution. The most surprising part was that her co-author always communicated throughout the narrative. It wasn't merely about the storyline involving David and Chelsie, the character; the responses and anti-responses between the authors also maintained a constant dialogue involving David and Chelsie, the author!

But now everyone insisted she had been writing those portions and then forgetting about them. How could that be possible? She knew she was perfectly sane. At the same time, she was aware that no intruder could have access to her laptop regularly. For that, a break-in would have been necessary! Did she have a serious mental disorder, then? Did she suffer from a split personality? Although Dr. Parker was quite clinical in his explanations, he didn't mention her condition's seriousness. Or, perhaps, he had revealed that to Brian, keeping her in the dark. She was vexed and edgy. Was she Chelsie by day and David by night? Was it a Doctor Jekyll and Mister Hyde scenario being re-enacted? Her head reeled the longer she thought about it.

And what about David, then? Even if he had written the anonymous portions, how did he do it — being dead for over half a decade? Is the spirit of the deceased present in the cottage? Is he — David — still there? Right now? Searching for his tragically estranged fiancé? Does he think Chelsie is Julia?

Never before had Chelsie believed in supernatural existence. But she was no longer sure of anything. As she lay on the bed, floating in a sea of confused consciousness, the possibility of David being very much real, even though he might be dead, flooded her senses. Only the previous evening had she left the manuscript at the crucial juncture where David had agreed to go on a vacation with the heroine. They would meet at a hotel in Florida, where they would experience a climactic sexual encounter. This was where the plot was destined to culminate. The union would reveal the true shades of her characters and tantalize the readers with flights of erotic fancy. Chelsie was confident her co-author had scripted the defining moment last night. She'd turn the laptop on after lunch and learn how the encounter went.

Quivering at the possibility, Chelsie felt a surge of desire rush through her veins. She was all alone in the cottage once belonging to David, lying on the bed where he must have explored many erotic possibilities with his betrothal – the girl who was, perhaps, Chelsie's alter ego! They must have engaged in countless explosive unions on such lazy summer days. Chelsie was thrilled at the possibility, in her sheer nightdress, revealing more than it draped, the man of her dreams might be standing next to her – soaking in her luscious charms through eager eyes that had long forgotten the joys of being alive! It was a bizarre thought, bereft of all reason, but, at least for the moment, she was devoid of all logic. The long wait for the man she'd searched for all her life was nearing its culmination. That man was a reality once, a man of flesh and blood with the same qualities that had endeared him to Chelsie – qualities she thought she had attributed to her in the novel, only to find he possessed them when he was alive. What did it matter if he was dead? To experience that one ultimate amorous explosion, Chelsie was ready to spread herself bare to David's spirit.

As waves craving swelled and ebbed through the most intimate bends of her anatomy, Chelsie pulled off her nightshirt and laid herself exposed to the scrutinizing gaze of her phantom lover. She imagined David would yank off his olive briefs and take Chelsie in the novel, rough and eager! As she conjured vivid images of the two characters riding the crests of pleasure together and surfing the troughs of unfathomable thrills, Chelsie the author – now at one with Chelsie the character – spread her legs in wanton delight. She felt she was being prodded under the lustful gaze of the phantom existence that permeated the room… the house… the entire countryside! Yes, David was the reason why she was here. It was his unrequited love that had drawn her to this place. Lust and yearning reached a crescendo through a furious burst of autoerotic release; Chelsie melted in the throes of passion as a formless existence of masculine vigor engulfed her senses and pervaded her consciousness. With every pore of her body, she felt with all her nerves and veins how it was to be with David – her ultimate hero.

****

She turned on the laptop after lunch. Her senses were refreshed after the release, and she was anxious to find out how her co-author had scripted the climactic scene. It would be awesome to read what David wrote about the experience. She scrolled impatiently to the point she'd left off the day before. It was almost afternoon, and Brian would return from work soon. Chelsie wanted to read what her co-author had written and add her portion before he arrived. She didn't want to be distracted. She reckoned today was the day to conclude the novel – what remains unspoken in a romance after the characters have reached the ultimate depths of their relationship? She would complete the novel by evening and call Kevin to share the good news. There would be no need for a second draft or editor since she and David edited as they wrote. Chelsie felt relieved. This had been the most challenging novel of her career, and she was certain that with the invaluable input of her co-author, it would define the rest of her career.

Chelsie found the new chapter – as expected! It started with David heading to Florida by car. Meanwhile, Chelsie reached Florida alone. She had to fulfill some other requirements as dictated by the plot, and the co-author was correct in sending her to Florida separately. They had decided to meet at the hotel, and Chelsie was waiting for David to arrive. David drove his green Opel and, urged on by the impending meeting, went full throttle.

She read in rapt attention. His description of the road added a dynamic boost to the narrative. The way he juxtaposed description with passages depicting David's stream of consciousness was superb. It imparted a kind of momentum rarely encountered in the romance genre. As Chelsie continued, she felt a distinct rush of adrenaline in keeping with the pace of the text. She read with bated breath until she arrived at the penultimate paragraph, where David's car lost control, skipped a lane, and rammed head-on into a truck on the other side of the road.

Senses numbed, she panned down to the last paragraph in disbelief.

"The green Opel lay overturned on the gray asphalt, its belly helplessly exposed to the merciless midday sun. The nose of the car was completely smashed.

The windshield lay shattered in a thousand shimmering crystal pieces adorning the dull tarmac, quickly turning a gory crimson. The truck had swerved widely and, even after being hit, managed to drive off — leaving the scene of catastrophe in utter silence. Vast groves of citrus stretched on either side of the road. Not a soul was in sight. The driver of the Opel, urged on by the call of life until moments ago, now lay lifeless inside the crumpled cabin. His intense eyes gazed incredulously at an azure sky stretched across the horizon. The front wheels of the car kept on spinning meaninglessly. They would soon cease as well."

CHAPTER 19

It must have been evening. The only light was from the laptop screen. It cast a glow as Chelsie sat illuminated by the blue halo. She read that one last paragraph for the thousandth time and couldn't make sense of it. She didn't care. At some point, she had abandoned the search for meaning. Was Brian home? It wasn't obvious. Was she crying? She didn't know.

How or why this happened, she didn't know either. Her co-author had always anticipated how she wanted the events to flow and directed the narrative down the desired path. He'd always fashioned the story towards a culmination which kept to the plot Chelsie had drafted. Even when passion made her deviate from the plot, her co-author brought the story back on track with expert editing. But what happened now was beyond her wildest dreams. It was a nightmare. No! It was the end of life!

Yes, it was the end of life because David was her life! A romance novel requires a happy ending, and the protagonist's death can never be a part of the scheme of things. Of course, she wanted this book to be different, but was this what she would have done? Chelsie didn't fear experimentation. But David was no ordinary hero. He was the man for Chelsie – not so much for Chelsie, the character, as for Chelsie, the author! How could he let her down? How could he deal such a fatal blow?

Chelsie got up from her desk and walked heedlessly ahead in the dark. She stumbled over the coffee table, lost balance, and toppled to the floor. Fortunately, she didn't hit her head, but she badly banged the big toe of her left foot. She couldn't care less! She rose from the floor and trekked in the dark again, heading straight for the living room. She yanked aside the curtains, and outside, it was dusk. She shrugged. Moving away from the living room window, she went to the bedroom. Fumbling in the dark, she reached inside her closet and pulled out the few items of David's clothing she'd taken from the trunk and kept permanently in her closet. They were bundled together: two checkered shirts, a pair of denim trousers, and a pair of olive briefs. She flung them all onto her bed and threw herself over them. She embraced the clothes, pressing them deep against her voluptuous bosom. She inhaled deeply to discover any distant whiff of manly cologne from the past still ensconced within their folds. Pulling aside her dress, she rubbed them over her naked skin. Then, tired and panting, she lay face down on the bed and broke into uncontrollable sobs.

She didn't know how long she cried. Outside, beyond their cottage and over the lake, the full moon appeared in all its glory. Moonlight streamed through the window and cast a silver pallor over the bedside table where foils and pill bottles stood readily by. When her eyes had run dry, Chelsie turned on her side and lay in silence, staring out the window. She could see a part of the reddish moon and the dark blue evening sky from her position in bed. She was exhausted; she needed to sleep. Stretching a trembling hand with much effort, Chelsie reached out. She needed the bottle with the little blue pills, as brilliant as the azure sky under which David lay dead after his car crashed. Blue signifies the sky, and the sky signifies freedom. She needed to be free. She needed to sleep. She was supposed to take these pills for three months – one each night before bed. They brought good sleep.

Fumbling and finally uncapping the bottle, Chelsie poured the remaining ninety-three azure pills into her mouth.

****

Brian met Bill near the town church on his way back. They walked home together. Bill had not heard from them since Brian handed Nick Carter's wallet to the police. He was happy to learn that no further intrusions had occurred. However, Bill knew nothing about Chelsie's illness.

Brian hesitated for a moment and then decided to tell Bill everything. This was the only person who had stood by them throughout their stay in the country, and Brian owed him a lot. He was genuinely concerned for their well-being. And somehow, through David and Julia, Brian felt Bill was now a part of the entire situation. He knew it would be unjust to keep this amicable elderly gentleman in the dark.

It was a long story and required a lot of explanation. It was also painful for Brian to recount portions that involved the dissolution of their marital harmony. As they neared Bill's home, he invited Brian in so that he could complete his account. Brian accepted the invitation. It was the second time he was telling someone after agent Kevin Firth. And he recounted things in greater detail to Bill than to Kevin. It seemed cathartic to him.

Bill was grave as he listened. By the time Brian finished, it was dark outside. Bill got up, switched on the lights, and settled again on the couch facing Brian. Both sat quietly for a long time as the grandfather clock ticked away. Bill broke the silence.

"Well, what do you want to do now?"

"I don't think I have many options," Brian said. "Chelsie is here to write the book. Despite her obsession with the co-author, she's making good progress. It's shaping up to be a good novel, and I don't think we should interfere with that. The best support I can give is ensuring she completes her work peacefully."

"How long will it take for her to finish the thing?"

"I think the first draft will be done soon."

"Do you plan to return to the city afterward?"

"Chelsie seems to have no plans now – either of staying or returning. But given her current frame of mind, I don't think she'd be too eager to leave the house where David lived."

"But that is precisely the problem. You need to take her away."

"If you want my view, I am inclined to go back," Brian said. Then he paused and resumed again, "And there lies the irony! I love the countryside, and I especially love this place. This job at the school is also to my liking. Yet I want to return now while Chelsie – the urban girl – wants to stay put!"

"Hmm." Bill let out a long sigh. After silence, he asked, "Do you really believe David's spirit is still around?"

Brian raised his eyes and stared at Bill's face for a long time. Then, with unusual firmness, he replied, "No, I don't. And please don't trouble yourself with such thoughts. Please, Bill!"

Then Brian stood. "It's getting late. I wouldn't say I like to keep Chelsie alone for too long. Perhaps I'll leave the job until Chelsie is fit again."

"That's a good idea," Bill nodded.

****

As he neared the cottage, Brian saw it was dark inside and figured Chelsie must be in bed. Not wishing to spoil her drug-induced sleep, Brian unlocked the front door carefully. Once inside, he was surprised to find the curtains drawn aside. Chelsie usually pulled them in place by late afternoon. How long had she been sleeping?

He hoped she'd had dinner, checked the kitchen, and saw dirty dishes on the counter. Satisfied with his inquiry, he walked across the hall and peeped through the study doorway. The room was empty and dark, save for the orange standby indicator of the laptop that glowed like a Cyclops in the desolate room.

Brian was relieved to find Chelsie had been working. She must have gone to sleep in the afternoon, he thought.

Then he noticed the coffee table on its side as he remembered something else. He walked with some urgency to the dormant laptop, tapped it back to life, and keyed in the password. He found the manuscript open at the fateful last paragraph.

Without reading it, Brian looked around the room and rushed towards the bedroom. By the moonlight, the messy and undone clothes lent Chelsie's inert form an appearance that portended some heinous torment. But as Brian switched on the light, the uncapped empty bottle of pills had its own tale.

****

It didn't take much to realize Chelsie was beyond human efforts. He sat holding her cold hand. The moon went higher and higher until it could no longer be seen through the window. Brian threw himself over her body and wept uncontrollably.

"Why did I want to play this game on you!" he sobbed.

Outside, the night progressed as the couple lay entwined in their last embrace – one blaming himself for a decision that led to a fatal end and the other silent. When Brian stopped cursing himself, he rose from the bed and walked to the living room. Pulling open a drawer, he fished out a folder and slammed it on the floor. The folder spewed a stack of notepad papers filled with copious jottings.

Brian sat amidst the clutter he'd caused and cried, "Why did I do it? Oh God! Why did I write this thing at all?"

Sitting on the floor, Brian leafed through the notes he'd made while planning the tenth Chelsie Crammer Romance narrative as its anonymous co-author. As a summer wind blew over the lake, Brian sat regretting staying up late each night – pretending to be David – and adding chapters to his wife's manuscript. As the moisture-laden winds came through the open window of the study and swayed the curtains, he lamented that he wanted to be the man his wife had always dreamed of. He remembered all the fantasies and quirks she'd shared with him and how badly he'd wanted her to have a fulfilling fantasy – for once.

A breeze playfully scattered the paper, and Brian sat and watched as his rough jottings for Chelsie's magnum opus danced around him. He had successfully impersonated the masculinity his wife had always wanted, but her obsession took things out of control. The coincidental similarity between Bill's son and the novel's protagonist and the fact that both were named David did complicate matters. However, Brian never imagined it would affect Chelsie psychologically. Later, alarmed at her neurotic obsession, he thought it was best to kill David. He'd hoped it would break the spell and shock Chelsie out of her imaginary romance. He wanted the novel to end with a jolt, but this wasn't the ending he had in mind.

****

The night moved on in its inevitable course. The forest stood dark and tall. The lake lay calm and inviting; nowhere else would he find such unprofaned serenity. It was his last repose.

Leaving all doors and windows wide open, Brian exited the cottage and walked towards the lake one final time, just like David had done five years ago.

THE END

THANK YOU!

Thank you for reading *Co-Author* I hope you enjoyed reading it as much as I enjoyed writing it. If you enjoyed this book, I would deeply appreciate it if you took a few minutes to write a review on Amazon.com. Even a short review would be fine. Reviews are vital to a book's success, and authors like myself enjoy reading what readers say.

Arthur M. Mills, Jr.

Arthur Mills

ABOUT THE AUTHOR

Arthur Mills has covered the world, both literally and figuratively. As a traveler, he's visited dozens of countries. As a reader, he's been able to visit a hundred more. And as a writer? He's been able to create a world all his own.

Arthur is the creator of *Branching Plot Books*, a book series devoted to the power of reader interpretation and interactive storytelling. Arthur has been able to pen novels to captivate people of all ages. Whether it's the horror of *The Empty Lot Next Door* or the interactivity of *The Crawl Space*, Arthur's primary goal in writing has always been to develop a deeper means of communication with the world—both real and imagined.

Arthur Mills

VISIT US ONLINE

- Website: https://www.branchingplotbooks.com
- Blog: https://www.branchingplotbooks.com/blog
- Community Hub: https://www.branchingplotbooks.com/members
- Facebook: https://www.facebook.com/BranchingPlotBooks
- Goodreads: http://www.goodreads.com/artmills
- YouTube: https://www.youtube.com/@BranchingPlotBooks
- Amazon Author's Profile: https://www.amazon.com/stores/Arthur-Mills/author/B0041DNH3E

Arthur Mills

Co-Author

Arthur Mills

Co-Author

Arthur Mills